P9-AEX-738

ISSUES THAT CONCERN YOU

Vegetarianism

Arthur Gillard, *Book Editor*

GREENHAVEN PRESS
A part of Gale, Cengage Learning

GALE
CENGAGE Learning·

Detroit • New York • San Francisco • New Haven, Conn • Waterville, Maine • London

Elizabeth Des Chenes, *Director, Content Strategy*
Cynthia Sanner, *Publisher*
Douglas Dentino, *Manager, New Product*

© 2014 Greenhaven Press, a part of Gale, Cengage Learning

WCN: 01-100-101

LIBRARY OF CONGRESS CATALOGING-IN-PUBLICATION DATA

Vegetarianism / Arthur Gillard, book editor.
pages cm. -- (Issues that concern you)
Includes bibliographical references and index.
Audience: Age 14-18.
Audience: Grades 9-12.
ISBN 978-0-7377-6936-4 (hardcover)
1. Vegetarianism--Juvenile literature. I. Gillard, Arthur.
TX392.V443 2014
641.5'636--dc23

2013042513

CONTENTS

Introduction   5

1. An Overview of Vegetarianism   9
   Douglas Dupler and Rebecca J. Frey

2. Humans Are Not Natural Vegetarians   20
   Nina Planck

3. A Plant-Based Diet Is Healthier than a
   Meat-Based Diet   25
   Hannah Vergara

4. Vegetarianism Is Not a Healthy Diet
   for Everyone   30
   Precious Williams

5. There Is No Moral Justification for
   Eating Animals   37
   Marc Bekoff

6. A Vegetarian Diet Is the Only Way to
   Reduce Animal Suffering   43
   Colleen Patrick-Goudreau

7. Sustainable Meat Reduces Animal Suffering
   More than Vegetarianism Does   48
   Jenna Woginrich

8. Vegetarianism Is Better for the Environment
   than a Diet of Animal Protein   53
   Lisa Hymas

9. Gentle Persuasion and Leading by Example
   Win More Converts to Vegetarianism than
   Militant Advocacy   58
   Shelby Jackson

10. Veganism Is Sometimes a Cover for an
    Eating Disorder   66
    Danielle Friedman

11. The Experience of Being Vegan and Vegetarian
    in High School   73
    Brittany Estes-Garcia

Appendix

   What You Should Know About Vegetarianism   80
   What You Should Do About Vegetarianism   85

Organizations to Contact   89

Bibliography   95

Index   99

Picture Credits   104

The roots of vegetarianism lie in ancient religious traditions such as Hinduism, Jainism, and Buddhism, all of which extol the virtues of nonviolence and compassion toward all beings. Modern vegetarians who choose the diet out of concern for the well-being of animals sometimes speak of *ahimsa,* an ancient Sanskrit word meaning "noninjury" that is associated with Buddhist, Jain, and Hindu principles of refraining from harming any living being. More recently, starting around the mid-eighteenth century, as science grew in influence, justifications for avoiding flesh in one's diet increasingly centered around the belief that vegetarianism provided many health benefits. Both in scientific circles and in the general population there has been skepticism of that claim, but gradual acceptance of the vegetarian diet has grown both in scientific circles and the population at large. Peggy Carlson, editor of *The Complete Vegetarian: The Essential Guide to Good Health,* points out that in the last several decades there has been a shift in the scientific studies of vegetarianism. "[Since the 1960s] the research has shifted focus from studies about the nutritional adequacy of vegetarian diets to the disease-prevention and therapeutic aspects of vegetarian diets."[1]

Of course, humans are diverse, and no one diet has been found to work well for everyone. In the 1960s the Dalai Lama, the spiritual leader of Tibet, adopted a vegetarian diet for almost two years for ethical reasons, making a stirring appeal for that dietary choice in a speech he gave at the Nineteenth World Vegetarian Conference in 1967:

> I do not see any reason why animals should be slaughtered to serve as human diet when there are so many substitutes. After all, man can live without meat. It is only some carnivorous animals that have to subsist on flesh. Killing animals for sport, for pleasure, for adventures, and for hides and furs is a phenomenon which is at once disgusting and distressing. There is no justification in indulging in such acts of brutality.

In our approach to life, be it pragmatic or otherwise, the ultimate truth that confronts us squarely and unmistakably is the desire for peace, security and happiness. Different forms of life in different aspects of existence make up the teeming denizens of this earth of ours. And, no matter whether they belong to the higher group as human beings or to the lower group, the animals, all beings primarily seek peace, comfort and security. Life is as dear to a mute creature as it is to a man. Just as one wants happiness and fears pain, just as one wants to live and not to die, so do other creatures.[2]

Over time the Dalai Lama found that his health was suffering. When he reintroduced meat into his diet on the advice of his doctors, he returned to his former healthy state. While he favors the practice of vegetarianism, he found that in his own case he needed some meat in his diet to be healthy.

Eating is not an optional activity; it is fundamental to survival, and what and how one chooses to eat can be a core component of personal or cultural identity. People often have strong beliefs about the way they and others *should* eat. As Mary Midgley, author of *Animals and Why They Matter*, points out, "The symbolism of meat-eating is never neutral. To himself, the meat-eater seems to be eating life. To the vegetarian, he seems to be eating death." Because of this, she notes that it is "hard to raise questions on the matter at all without becoming embattled."[3] Therefore, it is best to tread lightly when advocating for a particular type of diet. As the authors of *The Compassionate Diet*, Arran Stephens and Eliot Jay Rosen, state, "What we eat is of such importance to human progress and health, ecological balance, and animal welfare that food, like politics and religion, has become a highly charged and controversial issue. While diet is important, it is equally so not to injure the feelings and beliefs of others. Mutual respect is therefore highly valued and necessary, while holding fast to one's ideals."[4]

There are many issues in the world that urgently need to be addressed, and it is important to adhere to one's deeply felt beliefs. Vegetarianism is one lifestyle choice that aims to make a dif-

Author Mary Midgley says the symbolism of eating meat is not neutral. To the meat eater, eating meat is life. To the vegetarian, it is eating death.

ference. For Nobel Prize–winning author Isaac Bashevis Singer, "To be a vegetarian is to disagree—to disagree with the course of things today. Starvation, world hunger, cruelty, waste, wars—we must make a statement against these things. Vegetarianism is my statement."[5] Others address the same issues in different ways—for example, choosing to eat only humanely raised, environmentally sustainable meat, and/or reducing the amount of, but not eliminating, meat from their diets.

Although the number of practicing vegetarians in the United States remains a small minority of the population, it is clear that the various vegetarian movements throughout history have had a significant impact on the way people approach food. More people today are increasing the amount of fruits and vegetables in their diets and decreasing the amount of meat—whether motivated by the wealth of research showing health benefits of a plant-centered diet, by environmental considerations, or simply by a growing awareness of the many delicious vegetarian options to increase the diversity of one's meals. So-called semi-vegetarianism, or flexitarianism, in which people aim for a more vegetarian diet but still consume some flesh on occasion, is an option that appeals to an increasing number of people. Even among those who follow unabashed meat-centered, or omnivorous, diets, more people are attempting to do so consciously, choosing meat produced in more humane, sustainable ways.

This anthology offers a variety of perspectives on vegetarianism, as well as a thorough bibliography, a list of organizations to contact for further information, and appendixes containing facts and suggestions for further action for the interested reader or student researcher. The appendix titled "What You Should Know About Vegetarianism" offers facts about the problem. The appendix "What You Should Do About Vegetarianism" offers advice for young people who are concerned with this issue. With all these features, *Issues That Concern You: Vegetarianism* provides an excellent resource for everyone interested in this increasingly timely topic.

Notes

1. Peggy Carlson, ed., *The Complete Vegetarian: The Essential Guide to Good Health*. Urbana: University of Illinois Press, 2009, p. 13.
2. Quoted in International Vegetarian Union, "Famous Vegetarians: His Holiness the XIV Dalai Lama of Tibet." www.ivu.org/people/writers/lama.html.
3. Mary Midgley, *Animals and Why They Matter*. Athens: University of Georgia Press, 1984, p. 27.
4. Arran Stephens and Eliot Jay Rosen, introduction to *The Compassionate Diet: How What You Eat Can Change Your Life and Save the Planet*. Emmaus, PA: Rodale, 2011, p. 19.
5. Quoted in Stephens and Rosen, *The Compassionate Diet*, p. 35.

ONE

An Overview of Vegetarianism

Douglas Dupler and Rebecca J. Frey

Douglas Dupler is an editor of young adult books. Rebecca J. Frey has authored numerous articles for *The Gale Encyclopedia of Medicine*. In the following viewpoint Dupler and Frey describe vegetarianism both historically and in the modern era. According to the authors, vegetarianism originated thousands of years ago in various cultures around the world that advocated a vegetarian diet for religious or health reasons. In the United States, interest in this diet grew during the late nineteenth and early twentieth centuries, coinciding with widespread experimentation with novel health and dietary practices. Vegetarianism has been shown to be a healthy diet if certain precautions are taken, such as ensuring that necessary amounts of protein, vitamins, and minerals are part of the diet. Dupler and Frey note that a vegetarian diet has been shown to improve a wide variety of medical conditions and is often suggested by both conventional and alternative health practitioners.

Vegetarianism is the voluntary abstinence from eating meat. Vegetarians refrain from eating meat for various reasons, including religious, health, and ethical ones. Lacto-ovo vegetarians supplement their diet with dairy (lactose) products and eggs

Douglas Dupler and Rebecca J. Frey, Gale Encyclopedia of Medicine 4th ed., vol. 6, Copyright © 2011 Cengage Learning.

(ovo). Vegans (pronounced vee-guns) do not eat any animal-derived products at all.

Vegetarianism is recommended as a dietary therapy for a variety of conditions, including heart disease, high cholesterol, type 2 diabetes, and stroke. Vegetarianism is a major dietary therapy in the alternative treatment of cancer. Other conditions treated with a dietary therapy of vegetarianism include obesity, osteoporosis, arthritis, allergies, asthma, environmental illness, hypertension, gout, gallstones, hemorrhoids, kidney stones, ulcers, colitis, premenstrual syndrome, anxiety, and depression. Vegetarians often report higher energy levels, better digestion, and mental clarity. Vegetarianism is an economical and easily implemented preventive practice as well. . . .

Origins of Vegetarianism

The term *vegetarian* was coined in 1847 by the founders of the Vegetarian Society of Great Britain, but vegetarianism has been around as long as people have created diets. Some of the world's oldest cultures advocate a vegetarian diet for health and religious purposes. In India, millions of Hindus are vegetarians because of their religious beliefs. One of the ancient mythological works of Hinduism, the *Mahabharata*, states that, "Those who desire to possess good memory, beauty, long life with perfect health, and physical, moral and spiritual strength, should abstain from animal foods." The yoga system of living and health is vegetarian, because its dietary practices are based on the belief that healthy food contains *prana*. Prana is the universal life energy, which yoga experts believe is abundant in fresh fruits, grains, nuts and vegetables, but absent in meat because meat has been killed. Yogis also believe that spiritual health is influenced by the practice of *ahimsa*, or not harming living beings. The principle of *ahimsa* (non-violence) appears in the Upanishads (Vedic literature) c. 600–300 BC. Taking of animal life or human life under any circumstances is sinful and results in rebirth as a lower organism. It became a fundamental element of Jainism, another religion of India. Some Buddhists in Japan and China are also vegetar-

Yogis, people who practice yoga, are vegetarians because they believe that plant foods have life force, whereas the flesh of butchered animals does not.

ian because of spiritual beliefs. In the Christian tradition, some monks of the Catholic Church are vegetarian, and some vegetarians argue that there is evidence that Jesus and his early followers were vegetarian. Other traditional cultures, such as those in the Middle East and the Mediterranean regions, have evolved diets that frequently consist of vegetarian foods. The Mediterranean diet, which a Harvard [University] study declared to be one of the world's healthiest, is primarily, although not strictly, vegetarian.

The list of famous vegetarians forms an illustrious group. The ancient Greek philosophers, including Socrates, Plato, and Pythagoras, advocated vegetarianism. In modern times, the word to describe someone who likes to feast on food and wine is *epicure*, but it is little known that Epicurus, the ancient philosopher, was himself a diligent vegetarian. Other famous vegetarians include

[Renaissance artist and inventor] Leonardo da Vinci, [English physicist] Sir Isaac Newton, [Russian author] Leo Tolstoy, [early American philosopher and writer] Ralph Waldo Emerson, and [early American author and environmentalist] Henry David Thoreau. The twentieth century's celebrated vegetarians include [Indian statesman and religious leader Mohandas] Gandhi, the [famed English] physician Albert Schweitzer, writer George Bernard Shaw, musician Paul McCartney, and champion triathlete Dave Scott. [Physicist] Albert Einstein, although not a strict vegetarian himself, stated that a vegetarian diet would be an evolutionary step for the human race.

Vegetarianism in the United States

Vegetarianism in the United States received a lot of interest during the last half of the nineteenth century and the beginning of the twentieth century, during periods of experimentation with diets and health practices. Vegetarianism has also been a religious practice for some Americans, including the Seventh-Day Adventists, whose lacto-ovo vegetarian diets have been studied for their health benefits. Vegetarianism has been steadily gaining acceptance as an alternative to the meat-and-potatoes bias of the traditional U.S. diet. In 2009, the Vegetarian Resource Group conducted a poll that showed that 3% of the adult U.S. population identified themselves as vegetarians.

Several factors contribute to the interest in vegetarianism in the United States. Outbreaks of food poisoning from meat products, as well as increased concern over the additives in meat, such as hormones and antibiotics, have led some people and professionals to question meat's safety. There is also an increased awareness of the questionable treatment of farm animals in factory farming. However, the growing health consciousness of Americans is probably the major reason for the surge in interest in vegetarianism. Nutrition experts have built up convincing evidence that there are major problems with the conventional U.S. diet, which is centered around meat products that are high in cholesterol and saturated fat and low in fiber. Heart disease, cancer, and diabetes, which cause 68% of all deaths in the United States, are all believed to be influenced by this diet. Nutritionists have repeatedly shown in studies that a healthy diet consists of plenty of fresh vegetables and fruits; complex carbohydrates, such as whole grains; and foods that are high in fiber and low in cholesterol and saturated fat. Vegetarianism, a diet that fulfills all these criteria, has become part of many healthy lifestyles. In alternative medicine, vegetarianism is a cornerstone of dietary therapy, used in [traditional East Indian] Ayurvedic medicine, detoxification treatments, macrobiotics, the [Dr. Dean] Ornish diet for heart disease, and in therapies for many chronic conditions.

Transitioning to a Vegetarian Diet

Some people, particularly those with severe or chronic conditions such as heart disease or cancer, may be advised by a health practitioner to suddenly become vegetarian. For most people, however, nutritionists recommend that a vegetarian diet be adopted gradually to allow people's bodies and lifestyles time to adjust to new eating habits and food intake.

Some nutritionists have designed transition diets to help people become vegetarian in stages. Many Americans eat meat products at nearly every meal, and the first stage of a transition diet is to substitute just a few meals a week with wholly vegetarian foods. Then particular meat products can be slowly reduced and eliminated from the diet and replaced with vegetarian foods. Red meat can be reduced and then eliminated, followed by poultry and fish. For those wishing to become pure vegetarians or vegans, the final step would be to substitute eggs and dairy products with other nutrient-rich foods. Individuals should be willing to experiment with transition diets and should have patience when learning how to combine vegetarianism with social activities such as dining out.

The transition to vegetarianism can be smoother for those who make informed choices with dietary practices. Sound nutritional guidelines include decreasing the intake of unhealthy fats,

Vegetarian Food Pyramid

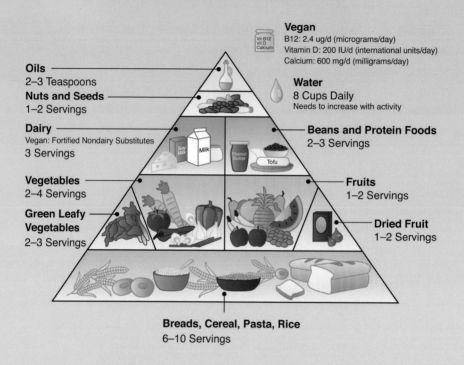

Vegan
B12: 2.4 ug/d (micrograms/day)
Vitamin D: 200 IU/d (international units/day)
Calcium: 600 mg/d (milligrams/day)

Oils
2–3 Teaspoons
Nuts and Seeds
1–2 Servings

Water
8 Cups Daily
Needs to increase with activity

Dairy
Vegan: Fortified Nondairy Substitutes
3 Servings

Beans and Protein Foods
2–3 Servings

Vegetables
2–4 Servings

Green Leafy Vegetables
2–3 Servings

Fruits
1–2 Servings

Dried Fruit
1–2 Servings

Breads, Cereal, Pasta, Rice
6–10 Servings

Taken from: "The Vegetarian vs. Meat Health Debate." *Tiana Star* (blog), August 7, 2011. www.tianastarblog.com /2011/08/07/vegetarian-vs-meat-health-debate/.

increasing fiber, and emphasizing fresh fruits, vegetables, legumes, and whole grains in the diet while avoiding processed foods and sugar. All people can improve their health by becoming familiar with recommended dietary and nutritional practices, such as reading labels and understanding basic nutritional concepts such as daily requirements for calories, protein, fat, and other nutrients. Would-be vegetarians can experiment with meat substitutes, foods that are high in protein and essential nutrients. Thanks to the growing interest in vegetarianism, many meat substitutes are now readily available. Tofu and tempeh are products made from soybeans that are high in protein, calcium, and other nutrients. There are "veggie-burgers" that can be grilled like hamburgers, and vegetarian substitutes for turkey and sausage with surprisingly authentic textures and taste. There are many vegetarian cookbooks on the market as well.

A set of guidelines for North American vegetarian diets is available from the American Dietetic Association and the Dietitians of Canada. The new guidelines are intended to promote variety within vegetarian diets and to meet the needs of different stages in the life cycle as well as to incorporate the most recent findings of medical research.

Precautions

One remaining drawback to the widespread practice of vegetarianism is the unusual taste or smell of many vegetables. A number of phytonutrients have a bitter, astringent, or acrid taste that they impart to products made from vegetables that contain them. Some experts think that people tend to reject such strong-smelling or bitter-tasting vegetables as turnips, cabbage, brussels sprouts, or broccoli because humans have been programmed in the course of evolution to associate bitter taste with poisonous plants. It is increasingly recognized that the major barrier to dietary change for the sake of health is taste. One recommendation for improving the taste appeal of vegetarian diets is more-frequent use of spices. In addition to pleasing the human palate, spices derived from plants have been shown to have chemoprotective effects, boosting the immune system, reducing inflammation, and fighting harmful bacteria and viruses.

In general, a well-planned vegetarian diet is healthful and safe; in the summer of 2003, a position paper endorsed by the American Dietetic Association and the Dietitians of Canada referred to vegetarian diets as "healthful, nutritionally adequate, and [able to] provide health benefits in the prevention and treatment of certain diseases." However, vegetarians, and particularly vegans, who eat no animal products, need to be aware of particular nutrients that may be lacking in non-animal-based diets. These are certain amino acids, vitamin B12, vitamin D, calcium, iron, zinc, and essential fatty acids. Furthermore, pregnant women, growing children, and those with health conditions have higher requirements for these nutrients.

Complete Protein

Vegetarians should be aware of getting *complete protein* in their diets. A complete protein contains all of the essential amino acids, which are the building blocks for protein essential to the diet because the body cannot make them. Meat and dairy products generally contain complete proteins, but most vegetarian foods, such as grains and legumes, contain incomplete proteins, lacking one or more of the essential amino acids. However, vegetarians can easily overcome this by combining particular foods in order to create complete proteins. For instance, beans are high in the amino acid lysine but low in tryptophan and methionine, but rice is low in lysine and high in tryptophan and methionine. Thus, combining rice and beans makes a complete protein. In general, combining legumes such as soy, lentils, beans, and peas with grains like rice, wheat, or oats forms complete proteins. Eating dairy products or nuts with grains also makes proteins complete. Oatmeal with milk on it is complete, as is peanut butter on whole wheat bread. Proteins do not necessarily need to be combined in the same meal, but should generally be consumed the same day.

Getting enough vitamin B12 may be an issue for some vegetarians, particularly vegans, because meat and dairy products are the main sources. Vitamin supplements that contain vitamin B12 are recommended. Spirulina, a nutritional algae, is also a vegetarian source, as are fortified soy products and nutritional yeast.

Vitamin D can be obtained from vitamin supplements, fortified foods, and sunshine. Calcium can be obtained in tofu, seeds, nuts, legumes, dairy products, and dark green vegetables, including broccoli, kale, spinach, and collard greens. Iron is found in raisins, figs, legumes, tofu, whole grains (particularly whole wheat), potatoes, and dark green leafy vegetables. Iron is absorbed more efficiently by the body when iron-containing foods are eaten with foods that contain vitamin C, such as fruits, tomatoes, and green vegetables. Zinc is abundant in nuts, pumpkin seeds, legumes, whole grains, and tofu. For vegetarians who do not eat fish, getting enough omega-3 essential fatty acids may be an issue, and foods such as flax, chia, or hemp seeds should be consumed, as well as walnuts and certain sea algae.

Vegetarians do not necessarily have healthier diets. Some studies have shown that lacto-ovo vegetarians often consume large amounts of cholesterol and unhealthy sources of saturated fat. Eggs and dairy products contain cholesterol and saturated fat (only animal products contain cholesterol), while nuts, coconuts, and avocados are vegetable sources of healthful saturated fats. Vegetarians may also consider eating only organically grown foods, which are grown without the use of chemicals, as another health precaution.

Research and General Acceptance

A vegetarian diet has many well-documented health benefits. It has been shown that vegetarians have a higher life expectancy, as much as several years, than those who eat a meat-centered diet. The U.S. Food and Drug Administration (FDA) has stated that data has shown vegetarians to have a strong or significant probability against contracting obesity, heart disease, lung cancer, colon cancer, alcoholism, hypertension, diabetes, gallstones, gout, kidney stones, and ulcers. However, the FDA also points out that vegetarians tend to have healthier lifestyles, so other factors may contribute to their better health besides diet alone.

A vegetarian diet, as prescribed by Dr. Dean Ornish, has been shown to improve heart disease and reverse the effects of atherosclerosis, or hardening of the arteries. It should be noted that Dr. Ornish's diet was used in conjunction with exercise, stress reduction, and other practices. The Ornish diet is lacto-ovo vegetarian, because it allows the use of egg whites and non-fat dairy products.

Vegetarians have statistics in their favor when it comes to presenting persuasive arguments in favor of their diets. They claim that a vegetarian diet is a major step in improving the health of citizens and the environment. Americans eat over 200 lbs (91 kg) of meat per person per year. The incidence of heart disease, cancer, diabetes, and other diseases has increased along with a dramatic increase in meat consumption during the past century. Many statistics show significantly smaller risks for vegetarians of contracting certain disease conditions. The risks of women getting breast cancer and men contracting prostrate cancer are nearly four times as high for frequent meat eaters as for those who eat meat sparingly or not at all. For heart attacks, American men have a 50% risk of having one, but the risk drops down to 15% for lacto-ovo vegetarians and to only 4% for vegans. For cancer, studies of populations around the world have suggested that plant-based diets have lower associated risks for certain types of cancer.

Reasons for Adopting Vegetarianism

Vegetarians claim other reasons for adopting a meat-free diet. One major concern is the amount of pesticides and synthetic additives such as hormones that show up in meat products. Chemicals tend to accumulate in the tissue of animals that are higher in the food chain, a process called *bioaccumulation*. Vegetarians, by not eating meat, can avoid the exposure to these accumulated toxins, many of which are known to influence the development of cancer. One study showed that DDT, a cancer-causing pesticide, was present in significant levels in mother's milk for 99% of American women, but only 8% of vegetarian women had significant levels of the pesticide. Women who eat meat had 35 times higher levels of particular pesticides than vegetarian women. The synthetic hormones and antibiotics added to U.S. cattle has led some European countries to ban U.S. beef altogether. The widespread use of antibiotics in livestock has made many kinds of bacteria more resistant to them, making some diseases harder to treat.

Vegetarians resort to ethical and environmental arguments as well when supporting their food choices. Much of U.S. agriculture is dedicated to producing meat, which is an expensive and resource-depleting practice. It has been estimated that 1.3 billion people could be fed with the grain that the United States uses to feed livestock, and poor nutrition is a major problem in world health. Producing meat places a heavy burden on natural resources, compared to growing grain and vegetables. One acre of land can grow approximately 40,000 lbs (18,000 kg) of potatoes or 250 lbs (113 kg) of beef, and it takes 50,000 gal. (200,000 L) of water to produce 1 lb (0.45 kg) of California beef but only 25 gal (100 l) of water to produce 1 lb (0.45 kg) of wheat. Half of all water used in the United States goes for livestock production. Vegetarians argue that the consumption of beef in the United States may also be contributing to global warming because of the large amounts of fossil fuels used in its production. The South American rain forest is being cleared to support U.S. beef consumption, as the United States yearly imports 300 million lbs (136 million kg) of beef from Central and South America. The production of meat has been estimated as causing up to 85% of the loss of topsoil of U.S. farmlands. A German researcher in the field of nutrition ecology has summarized the environmental benefits of vegetarian diets, saying, "Research shows that vegetarian diets are well suited to protect the environment, to reduce pollution, and to minimize global climate changes."

Despite the favorable statistics, vegetarianism does have its opponents. The meat industry in the United States is a powerful organization that has spent millions of dollars over decades advertising the benefits of eating meat. Vegetarians point out that life-long eating habits are difficult to change for many people, despite research showing that vegetarian diets can provide the same nutrients as meat-centered diets.

TWO

Humans Are Not Natural Vegetarians

Nina Planck

Nina Planck is the founder of the London Farmers' Markets and author of *Real Food: What to Eat and Why* and *The Farmers' Market Cookbook*. In the following viewpoint Planck argues that humans are naturally omnivorous, meaning eaters of both plants and animals, and that eliminating all animal sources of nutrition from the diet has deleterious health consequences—particularly for babies and children. She lists a number of essential nutrients that are not present in adequate amounts from plant-only sources, and claims that studies have shown lower levels of cognitive functioning in children who were formerly vegan and thus had no animal-based sources of nutrition during the critical developmental periods of their lives. While she acknowledges that a vegetarian diet that includes dairy and eggs can be healthy, she advises parents not to raise their children as vegans (i.e., total vegetarians who refuse to use any animal-based products in their lives).

The modern American is fierce about his or her right to choose a particular "lifestyle."

So it is with vegan diets for children. In 2007, when I argued in *The New York Times* that a diet consisting exclusively of plants was inadequate for babies and children, the response was dramatic, and at times, even vicious.

I believe that babies and children require a better diet. The American Dietetic Association asserts that a "well-planned" vegan diet—by which the experts mean one with many synthetic supplements—can be adequate for babies; I disagree.

The breast milk of vegetarian and vegan mothers is dramatically lower in a critical brain fat, DMA, as well as less usable vitamin B6, than is the milk of an omnivorous mother, opponents of vegetarianism claim.

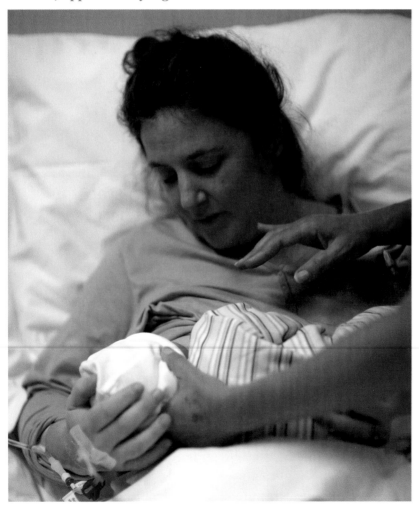

"Health Benefits of a Vegan Diet...
How the heck did this get here?"

Humans Are Omnivores

Nature created humans as omnivores. We have the physical equipment for omnivory, from teeth to guts. We have extraordinary needs for nutrients not found in plants. They include fully-formed vitamins A and D, vitamin B12, and the long-chain fatty acids found in fish.

The quantity, quality and bio-availability of other nutrients, such as calcium and protein, are superior when consumed from animal rather than plant sources. It's quite possible to thrive on a diet including high-quality dairy and eggs—many populations do—but a diet of plants alone is fit only for herbivores.

For babies and children, whose nutritional needs are extraordinary, the risks are definite and scary. The breast milk of vegetarian and vegan mothers is dramatically lower in a critical brain fat, DMA, than the milk of an omnivorous mother and contains less usable vitamin B6. Carnitine, a vital amino acid found in meat and breast milk, is nicknamed "vitamin Bb" because babies need so much of it. Vegans, vegetarians and people with poor thyroid function are often deficient in carnitine and its precursors.

The most risky period for vegan children is weaning. Growing babies who are leaving the breast need complete protein, omega-3 fats, iron, calcium and zinc. Compared with meat, fish, eggs and dairy, plants are inferior sources of every one.

Soy protein is not good for a baby's first food for the same reason that soy formula is not good for newborns. It's a poor source of calcium, iron and zinc—and much too high in estrogen. It also lacks adequate methionine, which babies and children need to grow properly. Lastly, soy damages the thyroid, which compromises immunity and stunts growth.

A Vegetarian Diet Is Dangerous for Children

Vegans may believe it's possible to get B12 from plant sources like seaweed, fermented soy, spirulina and brewer's yeast. Alas, these foods contain mostly B12 analogs, which, according to the health writer Chris Kresser, "block intake of and increase the need for true B12," a vital nutrient for mental health.

Mr. Kresser argues that this is one reason studies consistently show that up to 50 percent of long-term vegetarians and 80 perent of vegans are deficient in B12. "The effects of B12 deficiency on kids are especially alarming," he writes. "Studies have shown that kids raised until age 6 on a vegan diet are still B12 deficient even years after they start eating at least some animal products." In one study, the researchers found "a significant association" between low B12 levels and "fluid intelligence, spatial ability and short-term memory." The formerly vegan kids scored lower than omnivorous kids every time.

The greatest error of modern industrial life, which celebrates the lab and technology, is our love affair with the facsimile. It is time to face the music. Some things cannot be replaced. Real food is one.

You may choose to be a vegan. Your baby doesn't have that luxury. Let her grow up omnivorous and healthy. Then watch her exercise her own freedom of choice with justifiable pride.

THREE

A Plant-Based Diet Is Healthier than a Meat-Based Diet

Hannah Vergara

Hannah Vergara is a social media marketer based in Ohio. In the following selection Vergara asserts that a plant-based diet is much healthier than a diet based on meat. The author cites a study conducted in Denmark during World War I, when the entire population had to sharply reduce its consumption of meat for a period of time; during that interval, various health measures improved significantly throughout the nation. Another study, conducted by a scientist at the University of Kentucky, found significant improvement in diabetics who switched from a meat-based diet to a vegetarian diet. Vergara says it is not essential to remove all sources of animal protein from the diet to achieve improved health, but she suggests limiting meat consumption and making plant foods central to one's diet.

Changing the food that we eat can substantially change the way we look and feel. It is a common misconception in American culture that more protein equals more muscle and less fat. With American obesity at an all time high, it is important to have a good balance of appropriate vitamins and minerals in order to lead long, healthy lives.

The Human Body: Biology at Its Finest

Let's begin with the basics and examine the human body in a physical, anatomical sense. Humans are most closely related to primates with an estimated 99.4 percent of our DNA sequence shared with the chimpanzee. Our hands, teeth and bodies, similar to the primates, are designed for picking up utensils and grinding up plant matter. Compare that to a species of carnivore, such as the lion, that has the claws necessary to rip into flesh, and sharp fangs perfect for hunting and devouring animals. The design of each individual species has adapted over time to favor specific traits in the means of survival.

A further examination of our body design amplifies the substantial link between diet and health. For instance, the human liver has a low tolerance for uric acid, which is a by-product of meat, whereas the liver of a carnivorous lion contains uricase, an enzyme used to break down uric acid. Additionally, the human intestine is around thirty feet long; a length that provides adequate time for our bodies to absorb all the nutrients of broken down plant matter. In contrast, a lion has a shorter intestine designed for quickly getting rid of the acidic waste that animal protein produces.

Think about the source of the juicy protein steak you eat for dinner; the cow builds its large muscle from eating grass and absorbing plant protein. So, what are the effects of a culture that continuously over-consumes animal protein?

Meat Consumption Has Negative Effects on Health

Studies have shown that animal-based food diets show a strong association with incidence of cancer, heart disease and other illnesses. The digestion of protein creates different toxins in our body, which are subsequently absorbed into our blood stream and colon, eventually circulating throughout our entire system and clogging our bodies with by-products.

During World War I, a national experiment in vegetarianism involving three million citizens of Denmark had remarkable findings. Denmark was cut off from all imports of food because of the Allied blockade [the stoppage of maritime food and raw materials transports by the Allied Powers (Great Britain, Russia, France,

Vegetarians Versus Nonvegetarians

According to data from an ongoing study presented by lead researcher Gary Frase at the Academy of Nutrition and Dietetics 2012 Food and Nutrition Conference & Expo, male and female vegetarian members of the Seventh-day Adventist church in California live significantly longer than nonvegetarian Californians.

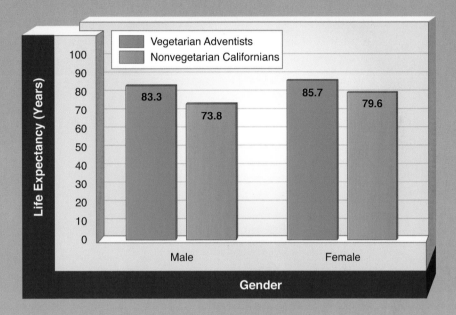

Taken from: Poonam Gupta. "Vegetarianism Can Reduce Your Risk of Death Over 30% and Add 9 Years to Your Life." *The Idealist*, May 4, 2013. http://idealistrevolution.blogspot.com/2013/05/vegetarianism–can–reduce–your–risk–of.html.

Italy, and the United States) into enemy Germany, Austria-Hungary, and Turkey]. To keep the population from starving, the citizens were forced to stop feeding grain to livestock. During the time food was limited, the death rate from disease decreased over 34 percent when compared to the figures from the preceding 18 years. When the war ended, the death rate rose again to almost perfect mathematical precision. Interestingly, similar cases were reported in Britain when a significant decrease in meat consumption occurred during World War II.

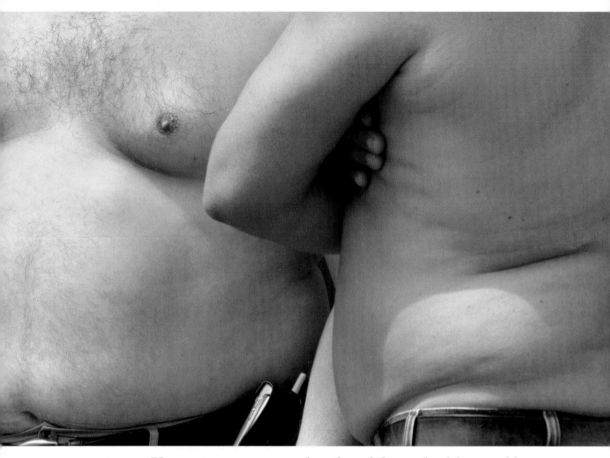

Vegetarians promote a plant-based diet as healthier and less prone to causing obesity than a meat-based diet.

Other compelling lab studies illustrate the positive benefits of plant-based proteins. For instance, Dr. James Anderson, of the University of Kentucky, conducted an experiment with 25 Type 2 diabetics. For one week, the patients were to eat a diet recommended by the American Diabetes Association. In the three weeks following, the patients had a diet constructed mainly of plant-protein and little meat. By the end of the experiment 24 out of 25 of the patients with Type 2 diabetes no longer needed insulin shots, and their blood cholesterol had dropped considerably. Since 2000, the rate of Type 2 diabetes has increased dramatically among younger adolescents, and continues to skyrocket along with obesity. Both diseases go hand-in-hand, and switching to plant protein provides a quick fix for both.

Understanding Plant Protein

Protein may be one of the most poorly understood food groups. Calorie for calorie, plant food contains almost twice as much protein as meat. The long chains of amino acids that make up proteins are utilized by our bodies. These amino acid chains link to form different combinations of building blocks, and our bodies use them in different functions, such as making antibodies and hormones or maintaining cell growth.

There are eight essential amino acids needed to create a complete protein. We need to obtain these crucial eight from the food we eat because our bodies cannot manufacture them. The eight essential amino acids are: phenylalanine, valine, lysine, leucine, isoleucine, tryptophan, threonine and methionine. An abundance of these amino acids can be found in fruits and vegetables. Leafy greens such as spinach and romaine, for instance, are prime sources of amino acids, and should be a daily part of our diets. Raw nuts and seeds are also great calorie-dense sources of protein.

Focusing our diet on plant-based protein helps naturally balance our body's biochemistry with alkaline-heavy foods. Clearing our system of acidic toxins frees up energy wasted on digestion redirecting it to weight loss and efficient aging. Not to say that animal protein should be completely cut out of our diet; instead, eat it in moderation. A maximum of once a day can provide us with enough energy to efficiently digest all protein, but try to eat heavier meals later in the evening.

Eat vegetables every day, and let's lead America to a healthier future. Instead of opening a bag of potato chips, bake some zucchini slices or steam an artichoke! There are plenty of healthy snacks that can nutritionally feed our hunger and create an overall more beautiful self.

FOUR

Vegetarianism Is Not a Healthy Diet for Everyone

Precious Williams

> Precious Williams is an author and former contributing editor at *Elle* and *Cosmopolitan* magazines. In the following viewpoint Williams argues that some people need meat in their diet in order to be healthy. She cites health experts who say that vegetarianism does not suit everybody; some people will not thrive unless they have some animal-based protein in their diet. The author describes how her health deteriorated after becoming vegan in college. No matter how she tried to adjust her diet and make it as healthful as possible, she kept feeling worse. Finally, she was diagnosed with anemia—a condition in which the body does not produce enough red blood cells or hemoglobin—and advised by her doctor to eat meat to resolve the problem. Eventually Williams took that advice and immediately noticed an improvement. Since renouncing vegetarianism, she reports feeling much more healthy and energetic.

Last week [in early April 2012], after 12 years of strict vegetarianism, I tucked into an oozing pink slab of sirloin steak. By the time the meat reached my plate, I hadn't eaten a morsel of meat during my entire adult life.

The idea of going vegetarian had hit me—literally—one morning during my first year at Oxford. On my way to a lecture, I was bashed in the face by a blood-caked dead pig that was dangling outside a butcher's shop. Already feeling hung-over and fragile, I promptly threw up and vowed never to eat meat again.

That evening, while my friends dined on beef Wellington at Formal Hall, I nibbled smugly on sautéed spinach with a side dish of broccoli. I had become revolted by meat when I was 10 and a classmate at school informed me that sausages (which I loved then) were made of pig testicles and wrapped in slivers of intestine.

Despite my horror at this, I continued eating meat and simply made a huge effort not to associate sausages with pigs or hamburgers with cows. But once I'd left home (where everybody ate meat and lots of it, at every meal) and started university, I felt keen to assert my newfound independence.

Going Vegan

I became a vegan overnight—and found this surprisingly easy, mainly because I naturally hate the foods that veganism forbids: eggs and dairy products. Then I moved to New York, home of the obscure food fad, and I immediately upgraded from veganism to macrobiotics—the brown rice and seaweed diet that reputedly keeps [actress] Gwyneth Paltrow and [singer] Madonna slim and serene.

Sadly, macrobiotics didn't really work for me. I ended up looking pale and feeling immensely hungry. I decided that the reason I felt washed out was because my diet, despite being organic and meat-free—wasn't healthy enough. So I cut out sugar, white bread, white rice, pasta, dairy products and wheat and, after reading that fashion designer Donna Karan was following a "raw food" diet—I stopped cooking my vegetables.

Karan had apparently lost a stone and a half [21 pounds/9.5kg] and gained loads of energy by eating raw vegetables and "sprouted" grains. I tried it and gained half a stone [7 pounds/3kg] and felt so extraordinarily sleepy that I could barely stagger to the local organic supermarket to buy my vegetables. Why, I wondered, did

Many nutritionists claim that red meat is the only source of easily assimilated dietary iron. According to the Centers for Disease Control and Prevention, 11 percent of women of childbearing age in America are iron deficient.

my friends who lived on pizza, pasta and hamburgers look so much healthier than me?

By this time, vegetarianism had become a huge part of my identity. I frequented health food shops, secretly looked down on people who ate meat, thinking them unenlightened and Neanderthal. I fantasised that I was doing wonderful things for my health by rejecting meat.

Negative Health Effects of Vegetarianism

The truth was that with each slightly more extreme variation of vegetarianism I tried, I grew slightly weaker, more lethargic, more depressed and—worse still—slightly fatter.

Every time I had a late night, I seemed immediately to get a cold afterwards. Often, I'd faint during the first day of my period each month. I felt ravenously hungry immediately after I'd eaten.

No amount of chickpeas, tofu, vegetables, fruit or lentils seemed potent enough to fill me up. When I looked at my reflection in the bathroom mirror I would be disgusted by how pale I looked. Even my tongue and lips looked pale.

I consulted my GP [general practitioner], who did a blood test that confirmed I was anaemic. She suggested that I give up vegetarianism, because, she claimed, red meat is the only easily assimilated source of dietary iron. In being anaemic, I was far from alone. According to the Centers for Disease Control and Prevention, 11 per cent of women of childbearing age in America are iron deficient.

As well as making you feel weak and tired, anaemia apparently gradually undermines your intellectual performance. "Women especially need to know this is actually affecting their brain and the way they're thinking," says Laura Murray-Kolb, a postdoctoral fellow at Penn State University.

Some Bodies Need Meat

I decided to persevere with vegetarianism anyway (although I did buy iron tablets, which didn't seem to do much good). Then, a few months ago, something strange happened. While shopping for my groceries at the local deli, I started lingering by the organic meat counter, stealing surreptitious glances at slabs of marbled beef and chunky lamb chops. I was like a little girl eyeing the glamorous clothes in her mother's wardrobe.

Around the same time, I read that [model and actress] Elizabeth Hurley was following something called the Blood Type Diet, started by a naturopath called Dr D'Adamo who claimed that there was no such thing as a one-size-fits-all healthy diet. In short, vegetarianism simply couldn't work for everybody.

D'Adamo claims that it all boils down to your blood group: people whose blood group is A can thrive as vegetarians and shouldn't eat any meat, while those of blood group O can't thrive without red meat. My blood group is O. I suddenly started to feel that meat, the only thing I hadn't tried eating in recent years, was the missing link to good health.

"There are certain people who simply need meat in order to thrive," says Meg Richichi, a New York doctor of Oriental Medicine. "I can look at people and tell that vegetarianism simply won't work for them. Chinese medicine dictates everything in moderation, including red meat."

A Return to Meat Consumption

And so, . . . while shopping for organic vegetables at Dean & Deluca in Manhattan, I decided to buy a steak. Looking at the vast bloody array of tenderloins, sirloins and ribeyes, I felt dizzy and overwhelmed.

Finally, I pointed at any old steak, said: "Give me half a pound of that" (nobody in New York ever says "please") and scuttled to the checkout, feeling slightly sordid.

When I got my parcel of steak home, I put it on the kitchen table, unwrapped it carefully and stared at it. I felt as though I had just brought home something dangerous, something that I had no idea how to use: like a gun.

My steak (medium rare and served with organic asparagus) was delicious. I felt daring and grown-up as I ate it. I'd expected to want to throw up at the first bite, but instead I felt satiated and bubbling with energy. Two days later, I had a small, organic lamb chop for lunch and the following day, a leg of corn-fed chicken.

Life After Vegetarianism

By the end of the week, I felt overwhelmingly full of life. My tongue was pink again and when I went to the gym I was able to run for 40 minutes without stopping, instead of flaking out after 20.

Since re-establishing myself as a carnivore, I've also lost 5lb in one week, perhaps because after eating a meal that contains meat I don't feel hungry again until the next meal-time.

World's Biggest Meat Eaters 2007, in Kilograms per Person

The United States has one of the highest rates of meat consumption per person on earth, exceeded only by Luxembourg.

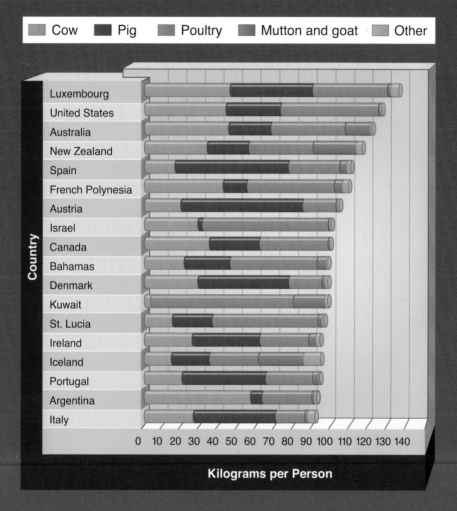

Kilograms per Person

Taken from: "Kings of the Carnivores." *The Economist Online*, April 30, 2012. www.economist.com/blogs/graphic detail/2012/04/daily-chart-17.

My vegetarian friends are, of course, horrified. I agree that it's a drastic leap, but I love making snap decisions and I love testing my willpower.

When I decided to give up smoking four years ago, I simply opened my sitting-room window, tossed a full pack of Marlboro Lights out on to the street, closed the window and never smoked again. Of course, everyone agrees that smoking is bad for you.

But the best health decision I've ever made was giving up vegetarianism.

FIVE

There Is No Moral Justification for Eating Animals

Marc Bekoff

Marc Bekoff is a former professor of ecology and evolutionary biology at the University of Colorado, Boulder. He cofounded Ethologists for the Ethical Treatment of Animals and is the author of *The Animal Manifesto: Six Reasons for Expanding Our Compassion Footprint*. In the following viewpoint Bekoff argues that eating animals is always morally wrong. He rejects compassionate, sustainable meat production as a moral alternative to vegetarianism because no matter how kindly the animal was treated while it was alive, killing it is not a compassionate act. He says that animals such as chickens and cows have deep emotional lives and rich social connections, and do not want to be killed any more than humans do. Bekoff points out that carnivorous animals are not capable of morality and hence cannot choose not to kill on moral grounds. Humans, as moral agents, have the capacity and responsibility to avoid killing, Bekoff maintains.

Eating Animals by Nicolette Hahn Niman, a livestock rancher, with help from deer hunter Tovar Cerulli and butcher Joshua Applestone, caught my eye because, at first, I thought this essay was authored by Jonathan Safran Foer, who wrote a best-selling book with the same title. While Niman and her friends do rightly argue against consuming factory-farmed animals—who live utterly horrible lives from the time that they're born to the time that they're transported to slaughterhouses and barbarically killed—these three born-again carnivores, all former vegetarians or vegans, now proudly eat animals and think that it's just fine to do so. They gloss over the fact that even if the animals they eat are "humanely" raised and slaughtered, an arguable claim, they're still taking a life. These animals are merely a means to an end: a tasty meal.

The Rich Emotional Lives of Animals

The defensive and apologetic tone of this essay also caught my eye, as did the conveniently utilitarian framework of the argument. The animals they eat were raised simply to become meals because Niman and others choose to eat meat. I like to say that whom we choose to eat is a moral question, and just because these three now choose to eat animals doesn't mean that other people should make the same choice. Note that I wrote "whom" we eat, not "what." Cows, pigs, chickens, and other animals raised for food are sentient beings who have rich emotional lives. They can feel everything from sheer joy to deep grief. They can also suffer enduring pain and misery, and they don't deserve to have the good and happy lives provided by Niman and others ended early just so that their flesh can wind up on what really is a platter of death.

Wolves, lions, and cougars are not moral agents and can't be held accountable for their actions. But most humans know what they're doing and are responsible for their choices.

Cows, for example, are very intelligent. They worry over what they don't understand and have been shown to experience "eureka" moments when they solve a puzzle, such as when they figure out how to open a particularly difficult gate. Cows communicate by staring, and it's likely that we don't fully understand their very subtle forms of communication. They also form close and enduring relationships with family members and friends and don't like to have their families and social networks disrupted. Chickens are also emotional beings, and detailed scientific research has shown that they empathize with the pain of other chickens.

Although less than 1 percent of the US population identifies as vegan, interest in the subject has grown in recent years. The graph below represents the change in the frequency with which people have searched popular search engine Google for the term "vegan" from 2004 to August 2013. The "100" in the graph represents the peak search interest to date.

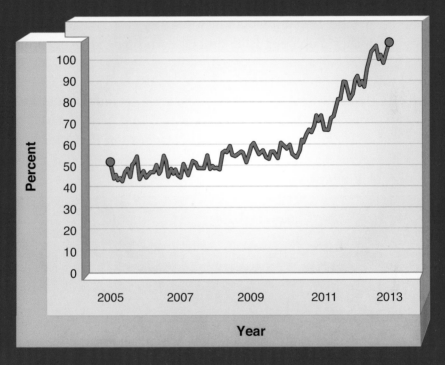

Taken from Google Trends, August 7, 2013. www.google.com/trends.

Choosing Not to Kill

Raising happy animals just so that they can be killed is really an egregious double cross. The "raise them, love them, and then kill them" line of reasoning doesn't have a meaningful ring of compassion. And this isn't mercy killing (euthanasia) performed because these animals need to be put out of their pain. No, these healthy and happy animals are slaughtered, and if you dare to look into their eyes, you know that they're suffering. If you wouldn't treat a dog like this, then you shouldn't treat a cow, a pig, or any other animal in this way.

As a field biologist who studies animal behavior, I feel that the authors' appeal to what happens in the natural world—"life feeds on life"—is an illogical justification for their food choices. I've seen thousands of predatory encounters. I cringe when I see them, but I would never interfere. Wild predators, unlike us, have no choice about whom or what they eat. They couldn't survive if they didn't eat other animals. And indeed, many animals are

The author points out that carnivorous animals are not capable of understanding morality, and hence cannot choose not to kill on moral grounds. Humans, on the other hand, as moral agents, have the capacity and responsibility to avoid killing, he says.

vegetarians, including non-human primates, who eat other animals only on very rare occasions.

Jessica Pierce and I wrote about how appeals to nature are misleading and illogical in our book *Wild Justice—The Moral Lives of Animals*. We argued that wolves, lions, and cougars, for example, are not moral agents and can't be held accountable for their actions. They don't know right from wrong. On the other hand, most humans do know what they're doing and are responsible for their choices. When it comes down to whose flesh winds up in our mouths, we can make choices, and in my view, eating animals is wrong and unnecessary, even when they are "humanely" raised and slaughtered. Let me add a caveat here because, as a world traveler, I do know that many people do not have the luxury of making a choice about their meals and must eat whatever is available to them. However, those who do have that luxury can easily eat an animal-free diet. And we can work to show others that a vegetarian or vegan diet can be very economical and healthy.

Expanding the Circle of Compassion

Niman and her friends also note that vegetarian and vegan diets have "never really taken hold." So what? This hardly means that we shouldn't try to do the right thing. They write, "The vast majority of Americans who do try vegetarianism or veganism— about three-quarters of them—return to eating meat. Rather than urging people to consume only plants, doesn't it make more sense to encourage them to eat an omnivorous diet that is healthy, ethical, and ecologically sound?" No, it doesn't. What it means is that these people should try harder and not give up just because it might seem difficult to change their meal plans. Perhaps they just need more time and encouragement from other vegetarians who can show them how easy it is to stop eating animals.

It's easy to add more compassion to the world and to expand our compassion footprint. Excuses such as "Oh, I know they suffer, but don't tell me because I love my burger" add cruelty to the world, even if the animals people are eating weren't raised on factory farms and killed in slaughterhouses. You're eating a dead animal who really did care about what happened to him or her. When I ask people how they can dismiss the fact that an animal was killed for their pleasure, they usually fumble here and there and offer no meaningful answer. When I ask them if they'd eat a dog, they look at me with incredulity and emphatically say, "No!" When I ask them why they wouldn't eat a dog, they can't really tell me, offering statements laden with dismissive phrases, such as "Oh, you know. . . ." Because I often travel to China to help in the rehabilitation of Asiatic moon bears who have been rescued from the bear-bile industry, people sometimes ask me, "How can you go there? Isn't that where they eat dogs and cats?" I simply say, "Yes, it is, and I'm from America, where they eat cows and pigs, who are no less sentient and emotional beings." Animals really are very much like us.

No matter how humanely raised they are, the lives of animals raised for food can be cashed out simply as "dead cow/pig/chicken walking." Whom we choose to eat is a matter of life and death. I think of the animals' manifesto as "Leave us alone. Don't bring us into the world if you're just going to kill us to satisfy your tastes."

SIX

A Vegetarian Diet Is the Only Way to Reduce Animal Suffering

Colleen Patrick-Goudreau

> Colleen Patrick-Goudreau is a vegan chef, author of *The Joy of Vegan Baking* and *On Being Vegan: Reflections on a Compassionate Life*, and host and producer of the podcast Vegetarian Food for Thought. In the following selection Patrick-Goudreau argues that no matter how animals are raised, it is wrong to unnecessarily kill them for food. She points out that relative to the expected life span of species that are raised by humans for meat, most animals on farms are killed when they are still babies, including millions of male chicks that are killed shortly after hatching each year simply because they cannot lay eggs. The author claims that there is no need for humans to eat animals for food for health reasons, and therefore there is no justification for the cruel practice of raising animals only to kill and eat them.

I have yet to meet a non-vegan who doesn't care about the treatment of animals bred and killed for human consumption. Even people who eat animal-based meat, aware on some level that the experience is unpleasant for the animals, will tell you they object to unnecessary abuse. Nobody wants to support cruelty, and nobody wants to believe they're part of it. Instead, they declare that they buy only "humane" meat, "free-range" eggs and "organic" milk, perceiving themselves as ethical consumers and these products as the final frontier in the fight against animal cruelty.

We bring into this world (only to kill) over 10 billion land animals every year just to please our palates and honor the status quo, yet we never question the absurdity of this societal ritual. Instead, we absolve ourselves by making what we think are guilt-free choices, failing to recognize the paradoxical impossibility of "humane slaughter" and also ignoring huge steps in the cradle-(domestication)-to-grave (our bodies) process.

Killing Animals for Food Is Inhumane

The unappetizing process of turning living animals into butchered body parts begins at birth and ends in youth—whatever they're raised for and however they're raised. Relative to their natural life span, most of the animals are slaughtered when they're still babies, as illustrated in the [accompanying] graphic. (And this graphic doesn't even include the millions of male chicks killed *upon hatching* at egg hatcheries every year. Males, after all, don't produce eggs and are thus worthless to the egg industry.)

When we tell ourselves we're eating the flesh and secretions from "humanely raised animals," we're leaving out a huge part of the equation. The slaughtering of an animal is a bloody and violent act, and death does not come easy for those who want to live.

The fundamental problems we keep running into do not arise merely from *how we raise* animals but *that we eat* animals. Clearly we can survive—and in fact, thrive—on a plant-based diet; we don't need to kill animals to be healthy, and in fact animal fat and protein are linked with many human diseases.

We know this. We know it instinctively, and the medical research supports it.

A Simple Answer

What does it say about us that when given the opportunity to prevent cruelty and violence, we choose to turn away—because

An Unnatural Life Span

Slaughtering animals when they are babies is standard, whether they are raised conventionally or in operations that are labeled "humane," "sustainable," "natural," "free-range," "cage-free," "heritage-bred," "grass-fed," "local," or "organic."

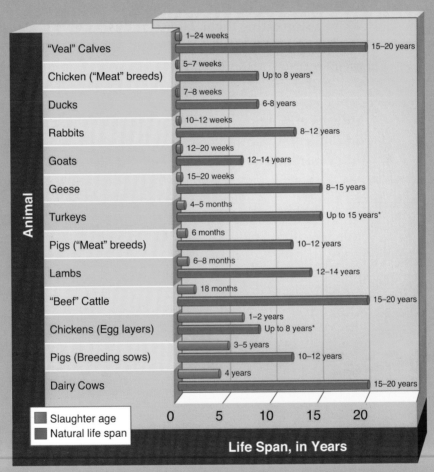

Animal	Slaughter age	Natural life span
"Veal" Calves	1–24 weeks	15–20 years
Chicken ("Meat" breeds)	5–7 weeks	Up to 8 years*
Ducks	7–8 weeks	6-8 years
Rabbits	10–12 weeks	8–12 years
Goats	12–20 weeks	12–14 years
Geese	15–20 weeks	8–15 years
Turkeys	4–5 months	Up to 15 years*
Pigs ("Meat" breeds)	6 months	10–12 years
Lambs	6–8 months	12–14 years
"Beef" Cattle	18 months	15–20 years
Chickens (Egg layers)	1–2 years	Up to 8 years*
Pigs (Breeding sows)	3–5 years	10–12 years
Dairy Cows	4 years	15–20 years

Life Span, in Years

*Most chickens and turkeys are bred to grow so fast that their bodies cannot endure very long. When not bred for consumption, chickens and turkeys can grow at a rate their bodies can sustain for many years.

Taken from: Colleen Patrick-Goudreau. "An Unnatural Life Span"; *Colleen Patrick-Goudreau: The Compassionate Cook* (blog), December 11, 2012. www.compassionatecook.com/writings/an-unnatural-life-span.

of tradition, culture, habit, convenience, or pleasure? We are not finding the answers we are looking for because we are asking the wrong questions.

The movement toward "humanely raised food animals" simply assuages our guilt more than it actually reduces animal suffering. If we truly want our actions to reflect the compassion for animals we say we have, then the answer is very simple. We can stop eating them. How can this possibly be considered anything but a rational and merciful response to a violent and vacuous ritual?

Millions of male chicks are killed upon hatching at egg ranches every year because they do not produce eggs and are thus considered worthless.

Every animal born into this world for his or her flesh, eggs or milk—only to be killed for human pleasure—has the same desire for maternal comfort and protection, the same ability to feel pain, and the same impulse to live as any living creature. There's nothing humane about breeding animals only to kill them, and there's nothing humane about ending the life of a healthy animal in his or her youth.

SEVEN

Sustainable Meat Reduces Animal Suffering More than Vegetarianism Does

Jenna Woginrich

Jenna Woginrich writes about farming and sustainable living and is the author of *Barnheart: The Incurable Longing for a Farm of One's Own* and *Made from Scratch: Discovering the Pleasures of a Handmade Life*. In the following selection Woginrich argues that choosing vegetarianism has no impact on reducing animal suffering because vegetarian consumers are irrelevant to the industrial farming practices that lead to widespread cruelty to animals. What *is* helpful, she claims, is to support sustainable, compassionate farming practices by purchasing meat from sustainable farms that treat their animals well. In that way, people demonstrate that they are willing to vote with their dollars by spending more for food that is from well-treated animals. Woginrich herself has gone from vegetarianism to raising and eating animals on her own farm. She says consumer choice is already having a positive impact, citing the rapid rise in farmers' markets as evidence of this trend.

I was a vegetarian for a long time—the bulk of my adult life, actually. When I realised how most of the steaks got to my plate (and how pumped-full of antibiotics and growth hormones they were), I put down my fork and took a vow to never be a part of that system again. My research into the brutal American factory farm system and its effects on the environment was a life-changing stumble down into the rabbit hole; I discovered a twisted world of assembly-line death camps, crippled animals, radiated carcasses and festering diseases. I don't have to get into the specifics, but clearly it wasn't a compassionate way to get my suggested 46 grams of protein a day. So I stopped eating meat, cold Tofurkey.

Supporting Sustainable Farming

Nearly a decade later I'm no longer a vegetarian. In fact, I couldn't be further from the produce aisle. Nowadays I own and operate a small farm where I raise my own chicken, pork, lamb, rabbit, turkey and eggs. I had a serious change of heart, and it happened when I realised my aversion to meat wasn't solving the animal welfare problem I was protesting about. My beef, after all, wasn't with beef. It was with how the cow got to my plate in the first place. One way to make sure the animals I ate lived a happy, respectable life was to raise them myself. I would learn to butcher a free-range chicken, raise a pig without antibiotics and rear lambs on green hillside pastures. I would come back to meat eating, and I would do it because of my love for animals.

Every meal you eat that supports a sustainable farm changes the agricultural world. I cannot possibly stress this enough. Your fork is your ballot, and when you vote to eat a steak or leg of lamb purchased from a small farmer you are showing the industrial system you are actively opting out. You are showing them you are willing to sacrifice more of your paycheck to dine with dignity. As people are made more aware of this beautiful option, farmers are coming out in droves to meet the demand. Farmers markets have been on a rapid rise in the US thanks to consumer demand for cleaner meat, up 16% in the last year [2010] alone.

Number of US Farmers' Markets, 1994–2012

Farmers' markets are a good source of local, sustainable, and often organic meat and vegetables, and are an increasingly popular alternative to industrialized farming. Between 1994 and 2012 the number of farmers' markets in the United States quadrupled.

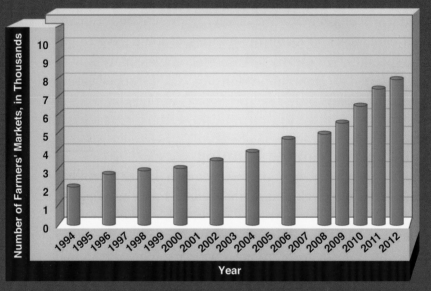

Taken from: Philip Bump. "Number of Farmers Markets up Almost 10 Percent Over the Last Year." Grist, August 3, 2012.
http://grist.org/news/number-of-farmers-markets-up-almost-10-percent-over-the-last-year/.

It's a hard reality for a vegetarian to swallow, but my veggie burgers did not rattle the industry cages at all. I was simply avoiding the battlefield, stepping aside as a pacifist. There is nobility in the vegetarian choice, but it isn't changing the system fast enough. In a world where meat consumption is soaring, the plausible 25% of the world's inhabitants who have a mostly vegetarian diet aren't making a dent in the rate us humans are eating animals. In theory, a plant-based diet avoids consuming animals but it certainly isn't getting cows out of feedlots. However, steak-eating consumers choosing to eat sustainably raised meat are. They chose to purchase a product raised on pasture when they could have spent less money on an animal treated like a screwdriver.

Making Animal Cruelty Bad for Business

"There is a fundamental difference between cows and screwdrivers. Cows feel pain and screwdrivers do not." Those are the words of Temple Grandin, the famed advocate responsible for making the meat industry aware of animal suffering. But how many of us consumers think of that steak in the plastic wrap next to the breakfast cereal and laundry detergent as just another object? A product as characterless as a screwdriver? We seem to be caught in a parted sea of extremes when it comes to how we see food—either we're adamant about where our food comes from, or completely oblivious. I don't think the world needs to convert into a society of vegans or sustainable farmers, but we do need to live

Temple Grandin (pictured), the famed animal advocate responsible for making the meat industry aware of animal suffering, notes that animals cannot be considered as just tools for human use: "There is a fundamental difference between cows and screwdrivers. Cows feel pain and screwdrivers do not."

in a world where beef doesn't just mean an ingredient; it means a life loss. I never thought of my beans or hummus like that. Now every meal is seasoned with the gratitude of sacrifice. For me, it took a return to carnivory to live out the ideals of vegetarianism. Food is a complicated religion.

It may mean spending more money, but the way small farmers raise their sheep, goats, cattle and hogs on pasture is the polar opposite of those cruel places where animals are treated like a cheap protein and "quality" is a measure of economic algorithms, not life. If cruelty is bad for business, business will simply have to change. When consumers demand a higher quality of life from the animals they eat, feedlots will become a black stain of our agricultural past.

I'm sorry, my vegetarian friends, but it's time to come back to the table. You can remain in the rabbit hole and keep eating your salad, but the only way out for good is to eat the rabbit.

EIGHT

Vegetarianism Is Better for the Environment than a Diet of Animal Protein

Lisa Hymas

Lisa Hymas is a senior editor at Grist, an environmental website, and writes about politics and environmental issues. In the following selection Hymas argues that vegetarianism has largely gone "out of style" lately, replaced by a trendy movement that believes vegetarians' switching to sustainable meat is a better ethical and environmental choice. She refutes that claim, noting that the meat consumed by the vast majority of US consumers is factory-farmed meat that has high environmental impacts such as excess water consumption and high emissions of the greenhouse gas methane. What is needed to change the status quo, according to Hymas, is not for vegetarians to switch to eating sustainable meat but for the vast majority of meat consumers to switch to at least occasional consumption of sustainable meat. She concludes that while consuming sustainable meat in small quantities is a better choice for meat eaters to make, vegetarianism is the most environmentally friendly dietary lifestyle.

It used to be that when I told a fellow progressive I'm a vegetarian, I would get one of three reactions: (1) an enthusiastic "me too!," (2) a slightly guilty admission of falling off the veg wagon, or (3) a voracious defense of the glories of steak.

These days, there's another increasingly common reaction: People look at me with a mix of pity and confusion, like I'm some holdover from the '90s wearing a baby-doll dress with chunky shoes and babbling on about [the music group] No Doubt. I can see what they're thinking: "You're *still* a vegetarian?"

At some point over the past few years, vegetarianism went wholly out of style.

The Sustainable Meat Fad

Now sustainable meat is all the rage. "Rock star" butchers proffer grass-fed beef, artisanal sausage, and heritage-breed chickens whose provenance can be traced back to conception on an idyllic rolling hillside. "Meat hipsters" eat it all up. The hard-core meaties flock to trendy butchery classes. Bacon has become a fetish even for eco-foodies, applied liberally to everything from salad to dessert, including "green" chocolate bars and "sustainable" ice cream.

All of which has led some vegetarians to give up their plant-based ways. But food fads aside, vegetarianism still has its place and deserves its due respect.

Let me state, for the record, that I wholeheartedly support the shift from factory farming to more sustainable meat production. Treating animals humanely, letting them eat what they're naturally inclined to eat, raising them without antibiotics and hormones, incorporating them into holistic farms [alternative farmer] Joel Salatin-style, and, once they're slaughtered, eating every last bit of them, nose to tail—that's all good stuff.

Most Meat Is Not Sustainable

But let's get real. Only a teeny-tiny fraction of meat in the U.S. is actually produced in any way that could conceivably be described as "sustainable"—less than 1 percent, according to the group Farm Forward—and only a teeny-tiny fraction of *that* is raised in the

Most of the meat raised in America comes with serious environmental impacts, from high water consumption to large land usage to excessive methane emissions and waste runoff.

super-duper-über-conscientious Salatin style. Most of the meat raised even by those trying to do it right comes with serious environmental impacts, from high water consumption to large land footprints to excessive methane emissions.

So it really gets my goat (ahem) when people claim it's more responsible to eat supposedly sustainable meat than to abstain from it—like the author of this facile [glib] article from *Food & Wine*, who pats herself on the back for convincing her husband to give up his vegetarianism:

> For Andrew and about a dozen people in our circle who have recently converted from vegetarianism, eating sustainable meat

Greenhouse Gas Generated to Produce 1 Kilogram of Protein

CO_2e (carbon dioxide equivalent) is a standard measurement used to account for all greenhouse gases that contribute to global warming/climate change. The chart below shows the amount of CO_2e released into the atmosphere in the production of 1 kilogram (kg) of various types of protein.

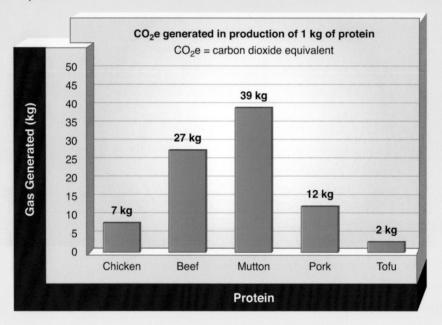

Taken from: Alwyn Marriage. "Politics on Your Plate." *alwynmarriage* (blog). http://alwynmarriage.wordpress.com/tag/vegetarianism/.

purchased from small farmers is a new form of activism—a way of striking a blow against the factory farming of livestock that books like Michael Pollan's *The Omnivore's Dilemma* describe so damningly.

Oh come on. You're not striking any more of a blow against Big Meat by buying your sustainable sausage at the farmers market than I am by buying my dried beans at the farmers market.

To nudge our horrific food system toward sustainability, we don't need vegetarians to shift to occasional consumption of ethically produced meat. We need the American masses who eat an average of half a pound of factory-farmed meat a day to shift to the occasional consumption of ethically produced meat. (Americans are actually eating a little less meat overall these days, no thanks to the meat hipsters.)

Vegetarianism Is the Best Environmental Choice

Eating truly sustainable meat, in modest quantities, is a fine thing. But it's not *better* than eating no meat—certainly not when we've got more than 7 billion people on a fast-heating planet competing to feed themselves via shrinking, oversubscribed cropland and increasingly limited, degraded freshwater supplies.

Yes, vegetarians can do better, too. Just as most meat-eaters, even green-leaning ones, consume at least some less-than-exemplary meat, most vegetarians eat some highly processed, GMO [genetically modified organism]–tainted, decidedly non-local soy products that wouldn't win any sustainability awards. And just as omnivores can focus on eating better meat, vegetarians can focus on eating better sources of protein. When vegetarians do aim higher, it's hard to beat them on the sustainability front—a non-soy-based, non-heavily-processed, local-focused veg diet is the definition of low impact.

In the end, vegetarianism—eating lower on the food chain, gobbling up fewer resources and less water—is still an ethical, environmentally friendly choice, just like it was in the '90s. Maybe even more so now, if you consider how our environmental, energy, and food challenges have compounded in the last two decades.

So, meat hipsters, drop that smug sanctimony. Sometime soon, bacon-spiked dessert will look just as outmoded as lentil loaf and baby-doll dresses—and vegetarianism will still be a good choice for my health, society at large, and our global environment.

NINE

Gentle Persuasion and Leading by Example Win More Converts to Vegetarianism than Militant Advocacy

Shelby Jackson

Shelby Jackson has worked as an intern for the Vegetarian Resource Group, a nonprofit organization dedicated to educating the public about vegetarianism and the interrelated issues of health, nutrition, ecology, ethics, and world hunger. In the following selection Jackson talks about how to effectively advocate for a vegetarian lifestyle, particularly with one's family and friends, illustrating her points with examples from her own life and those of other young vegetarians. She says trying to convince everyone to be vegetarian can be emotionally draining and counterproductive. Jackson notes that young vegetarians often encounter criticism and opposition from family and friends, but getting defensive and aggressive or harshly criticizing the meat-based diet of one's family and friends will not help persuade them. Instead, politely answering their questions and demonstrating by one's own example that one enjoys a healthy and happy lifestyle is more likely to gradually lead others to curiosity about and acceptance of vegetarianism.

Sometimes social pressures make being vegetarian a struggle. Growing up in Broken Arrow, Oklahoma, amidst a family of ranchers and a high school swarming with Future Farmers of America enthusiasts, veganism often set me apart from the rest of my community. Though it was difficult at the beginning, I would soon learn some tricks of the trade that would allow me to politely confront aggressive oppositions to my lifestyle choices. Upholding and smartly promoting vegetarianism began to feel natural and easy, and my assured confidence allowed me to persevere through the most heated of confrontations.

Some vegetarians are more inclined to activism than others, and it is important to recognize where you stand, and to choose your battles accordingly. If I attempted to convince every person who gave me trouble for being vegan, I would be an emotional wreck. Arguing about issues you care deeply about can be extremely frustrating, and it is important to realize that it is not always worth it. If you feel emotionally taxed, or have the feeling that your arguments for vegetarianism are chipping away at your well-being, take a moment to self-reflect. Realize that you most likely will not convince the pig farmer to become vegetarian, and that not everyone can be persuaded to change their habits. This does not mean you should give up; rather, you should target your efforts to an audience that may perceive your message more readily.

The Virtue of Patience

Patience is key. My mother was upset when I became vegetarian, but 6 years later she decided to adopt the diet herself. A relatively modest promotion of vegetarianism around the aggressively omnivorous is often the best approach to take. In high school, one of my tennis teammates, Morgan Chissoe, the daughter of a cattle rancher, made fun of my veganism nearly every day. Rather than getting into a heated argument every time Morgan did this, I would simply shake it off, offer a brief explanation of why I thought she was wrong, and aim a joke back at her. Two years into our friendship, she began asking me more detailed questions about my lifestyle choices and soon after became vegetarian. She explained to me how, at her farm, the mother cows' cries when their offspring were taken away often kept her up at night. I would have never guessed that this particular friend would become vegetarian, and that my lifestyle choices would eventually cause her to re-examine her own.

When asking Morgan how her family reacted to her transition to vegetarianism, she claims they saw it as a "phase," and often made jokes about her new dietary choices. A country girl whose family's dinners are often steak and mashed potatoes, Morgan had to endure verbal abuse from her family members at every family gathering. Having grown up on a farm and been around cattle her entire life, Morgan feels her family will never truly understand vegetarianism. Despite this, she claims things have gotten better: "My step mom regularly buys veggie patties and when she makes beans, she makes the vegetarian kind just for me." Her mother even started eating occasional vegetarian dishes after realizing the health benefits.

Setting a Good Example

Being vegetarian in an agricultural community, Morgan is continuously confronted with opposition. She does her best to answer their questions, but when she starts to feel disrespected, she states, "You have your opinion and I have mine and it's my life so I will eat what I want and feel good about it." Morgan claims that most accept this answer and if they do not, she simply leaves the conversation. Morgan's advice to a struggling vegetarian is to "hang in there because even though people do not agree with you, those close to you are likely to gradually come to respect your viewpoints." Morgan explains how one of her omnivorous friends always wanted to be vegetarian but was too overwhelmed by the community's love of meat. After becoming inspired by the way Morgan adjusted to her situation, she soon became vegetarian.

Sometimes such strong opposition stems from familial ties to meat industry occupations, or engrained cultural habits; other times, it could be from lack of understanding. Grace Afsari-Mamagani, a college student, claims that a meat-heavy diet is the cultural norm

PETA members, usually known for their militancy, here engage in a gentler means of protest by joining in the "National Veggie Hotdog Day" rally to promote vegetarianism.

for her Polish family. Because her mother insists that a vegetarian diet is a less healthy diet [than one with meat], Grace is sure to demonstrate that she knows what she is doing and has educated herself enough to understand how to create a balanced, varied diet. After becoming more informed, Grace's mother is more accepting of vegetarianism, and has noticed that Grace has become healthier and now eats a wider variety of food than she did when she ate meat. Always willing to explain and defend her decision, Grace realizes that "some people will probably never change their minds." For Grace, "That's okay: I can inform them, provide my viewpoint, and accept the differences." Grace believes that "sometimes you just have to let the criticism happen after you have done what you can; I always try to take it with a smile."

My grandmother, who has killed and prepared her own fish and chicken for a large part of her life, will never understand veganism. Even after I have explained countless times how important veganism is to me, I have caught her slipping animal ingredients into my vegan holiday pies. I have learned to supervise and help with foods she makes for me, and to bring my own meals when visiting. Some people will never understand veganism, and it is helpful to accept this and, like Morgan and Grace, move on rather than fixate and become frustrated by something that is unlikely to change. This is not to say that you should lose hope in convincing those close friends and family members that appear unlikely to change. It helps to be patient and mindful of the way you portray vegetarianism. Never make it look difficult and try not to complain about such things as lack of options at a restaurant. You want to portray vegetarianism as the easy, enjoyable, and worthwhile lifestyle that it is.

Inspired by Opposition

"'Surviving' in an Agricultural High School," an article written by past VRG [Vegetarian Resource Group] intern Veronica Lizaola, claims that attending a high school that was not accepting [of] vegetarianism "eventually reaffirmed and strengthened my beliefs." For Veronica, opposition to her dietary choices "served as the ultimate motivating force to inform others about a more ethical lifestyle." Instead of becoming discouraged when others try to bring you down, become inspired by their lack of understanding and the tremendous potential you have as a vegetarian. A vegetarian presence alone is enough to cause others to think about vegetarianism—and this simple act of thinking is often the first step to an eventual dietary conversion, or at the very least, a more informed and respectful view.

Debbie Schaefer became vegetarian at the age of 11. When Debbie first told her parents about her decision, they "started crying as though I had just confessed to some horrific eating disorder." Last Thanksgiving, her aunt purposefully cooked everything in turkey broth, and then scolded Debbie for being rude when she refused to eat anything. One of Debbie's teachers commented that all vegetarians are "self-centered, inconsiderate, and attention seeking." This teacher then attempted to get a rise out of Debbie by describing, in detail, how he had chosen a live dog at a restaurant in China, watched its slaughter, and then enjoyed consuming its flesh.

When asked how she overcame such opposition, Debbie says, "It's been a lot of trial and error." Debbie claims that she used to try to educate people as to why she became vegetarian, but then she came to the conclusion that "if someone isn't open to hearing it, then they are not going to." When answering questions about vegetarianism, Debbie simply responds, "I wanted to know where my food came from, and when I found out, I didn't like it." Debbie has found that this response helps guide those genuinely curious to do their own research, while not giving those eager to argue much to work with. Years later when Debbie asked her parents why they cried when she first told them, they said it was because they felt as if she was "rejecting their lifestyle choices—something they took rather personally—and worse, they couldn't understand why." Debbie feels that, although it has taken years, "they are slowly beginning to understand," and now only eat meat once or twice a week.

Harsh Criticism Is Counterproductive

Aulbry Freeman, a college student from a town with few vegetarians, became vegan in high school. Aulbry was so used to getting grief about vegetarianism that she was "automatically defensive, and wouldn't hesitate to tell people the disgusting truth about the food they were eating while they were eating it." A few of Aulbry's omnivore friends disliked her constant criticism so much that they began to distance themselves from her altogether. After a year's time, Aulbry realized that offending and disgusting people was not the best approach. Aulbry was reflecting the disrespect

In the following graph, compiled from information in a 2012 survey by the Vegetarian Resource Group, *primary reason* is the main reason respondents gave for being vegetarian/vegan. The *contributory reason* refers to a question that allowed respondents to give multiple reasons for being vegeterian/vegan.

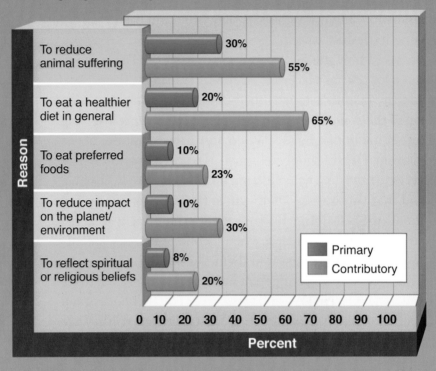

To reduce animal suffering — Primary 30%, Contributory 55%
To eat a healthier diet in general — Primary 20%, Contributory 65%
To eat preferred foods — Primary 10%, Contributory 23%
To reduce impact on the planet/environment — Primary 10%, Contributory 30%
To reflect spiritual or religious beliefs — Primary 8%, Contributory 20%

Reason / Percent

Taken from: "Consider Vegetarians." nxtbook media, May/June 2013. www.nxtbook.com/sosland/isb/2013_06_01/index.php?startid=20.

from her community back on to them; and often, the victims of her harsh criticism were those who deserved it least. When facing daily opposition against being vegetarian, it is easy to get sucked into unproductive methods of advocacy. Lashing out at anyone who eats meat or uses dairy products casts a bad image of vegetarians and does nothing to promote the cause. Rather than directing useless criticism back on to those who oppose you, or those whose lifestyles are different from your own, keep in mind that there are better ways to voice your concerns. Individuals are unlikely to become vegetarian, or even to respect it, when they are being criticized. The best approach vegetarians can take is to politely inform, as those willing to adopt a vegetarian diet must make the decision on their own.

When being rudely confronted about your lifestyle choices, keep in mind that these moments are prime opportunities for advocacy—because it is in this instance where a small amount of carefully executed effort can leave a lasting impression. An individual must be seen as credible for another person to sincerely take their words into consideration, so be careful to not offend. When it comes to family members and close friends, there is a fine line between activism and rudeness that is easy to overlook. Rather than offending those who are close to you, channel your frustrations and cultivate it through an intelligently constructed explanation. Stay positive, remain patient, and remember: you are always affecting change, even when it seems like you are not.

TEN

Veganism Is Sometimes a Cover for an Eating Disorder

Danielle Friedman

> Danielle Friedman is a graduate of the Columbia University Graduate School of Journalism and a senior editor at *Newsweek* and its new website, *The Daily Beast*. In the following selection Friedman argues that while most people choose vegetarianism or veganism for good reasons, in some cases it can be a way to cover up for an eating disorder such as anorexia. For people with an eating disorder, being vegetarian or vegan can provide a convenient excuse to avoid eating, since many foods contain animal products. In other cases, she notes, someone may choose to become vegetarian/vegan for good reasons but then find themselves progressively engaging in disordered eating habits over time. According to the author, if someone has a biological predisposition toward eating disorders, then any diet that restricts food choices can put them at risk. Choosing vegetarianism to lose weight also increases the risk of developing an eating disorder.

When Jill Miller reflects on her long, painful dance with veganism, anorexia, and bulimia, she remembers standing alone in her kitchen, binge-eating a tofu-cream pie.

These episodes of stuffing herself with whipped soy—when what she really wanted was a pint of Ben & Jerry's—stand out in her mind as a sign that her commitment to veganism was a cover for something darker. As do the many times that she turned down food with the seemingly innocent, even noble excuse that no one could argue with: Oh, sorry. I can't eat that—I'm vegan.

"No prime rib and Yorkshire pudding at New Year's with Grandpa," says Miller. "This happened at every family event."

Vegetarianism as an Excuse to Refuse Food

The shame, discomfort, and self-loathing represented by her eating habits defined much of her early life. When she was just 13, Miller became a vegetarian, in part for philosophical reasons, but mainly as an excuse to avoid her mom's New Orleans–style chicken-fried steak and jambalaya. As she forged a career in yoga instruction, she further restricted her diet by going vegan, all the while struggling with an eating disorder that she kept under wraps.

"I seized on the food theory of veganism to justify my desire to restrict," she told The Daily Beast. "It was a convenient way to eliminate fat and calories."

A breakthrough came shortly after she turned 30. She realized that the only way to fight her illness—and be happy—was to stop saying "no" to so many foods, and begin saying "yes." She's now an omnivorous yoga guru, starring in dozens of instructional DVDs, and she's never felt better.

As veganism moves from the fringes to the mainstream of American culture, with A-listers like [actress] Natalie Portman and [writer] Jonathan Safran Foer loudly endorsing it, more Americans are giving it a whirl. Five percent of people in this country identify as vegan, according to a 2002 Time/CNN poll. And for most, becoming vegan can mark a healthy shift toward wholesome eating and concern for the welfare of animals. But for those at risk of developing an eating disorder, it can mask or trigger an illness, providing a socially conscious excuse not to partake in family barbeques or dinners out with friends.

Most Vegetarians Do Not Have an Eating Disorder

According to Dr. Angela Guarda, director of the Johns Hopkins Eating Disorders Program, many vegans (and vegetarians) who enter her treatment center initially deny an underlying problem—only to later confess that their efforts to avoid animal products were really an effort to avoid food in general. "In most of our patients, the vegetarianism is in the service of the eating disorder," she said.

For this reason, Guarda and her staff try to dissuade patients from observing any form of vegetarianism while undergoing treatment, encouraging them to broaden their food repertoire to include some meat. Other eating disorder and nutrition specialists report similar approaches.

Dr. Marcia Herrin, founder of the Dartmouth College Eating Disorders Prevention, Education and Treatment Program and now a dietician in private practice, takes a stricter (if potentially problematic) approach: Herrin tells parents not to let their kids be vegetarian until they go to college, echoing that the diet can create a "ruse" that loved ones can't see through. "Most families don't have the time to prepare vegetarian entrées," she said. "What's at risk is the child's growth and development, and potentially an eating disorder."

Herrin may be onto something: A 2009 study in the *Journal of the American Dietetic Association* revealed that young adults aged 15 to 23 who reported being vegetarian were, at some point, more likely to have also engaged in unhealthy weight-loss behaviors like bingeing, purging, and using diet pills or laxatives. And surveys show that the prevalence of vegetarianism among eating-disorder patients is higher than in the general population.

It's important to note that for most of the country's roughly 3 million vegans, who don't consume or wear any animal products, their eating habits never veer into mental illness. Many consider veganism a lifestyle, says Annie Hartnett, an animal-rights activist and blogger for Change.org, or a protest against cruel farming practices. And studies have found that the physical benefits of

Eating Disorders and Vegetarianism

A study of ninety-three females with a history of eating disorders published in the *Journal of the Academy of Nutrition and Dietetics* in 2010 found that many of them were current or former vegetarians.

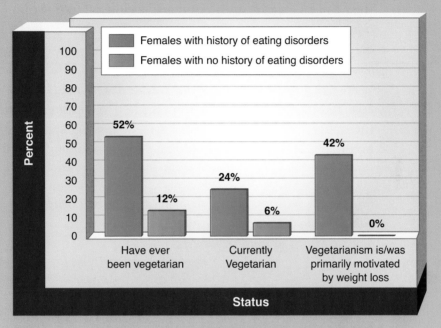

Taken from: Anna M. Bardone-Cone et al. "The Inter-Relationships Between Vegetarianism and Eating Disorders Among Females." *Journal of the Academy of Nutrition and Dietetics,* vol. 112, no. 8, pp. 1247–1252, August 2012. www.andjrnl.org/article/522212-2672(12)00627-2/abstract.

veganism, when observed in a healthy way, are extraordinary, including lowered risk of chronic disease, improved heart health, and increased energy.

Vegetarianism for Weight Loss: A Dangerous Motivation

Problems arise when individuals approach veganism primarily as a vehicle for weight loss, and indeed, more than ever, it's being marketed by certain proponents as an extreme diet. Last month [June 2010], actress Jessica Simpson tweeted that she's going vegan, along with drinking a popular weight-loss tea. While she later claimed the veganism isn't to shed pounds, tabloids have since treated it as if it were the next Atkins Diet [a longtime popular diet]. Then there's the bestselling *Skinny Bitch* series, a vegan manifesto in diet-book packaging. Even PETA [People for the Ethical Treatment of Animals] is guilty: This past May, the organization proposed placing an ad on the Great Wall of China, depicting an overweight American tourist, with the caption: "It's the Wall That We Should See From Space, Not You. Go Vegan."

At the most toxic end of the eating-disorder spectrum. "Pro-ana" [promoting anorexia] websites pitch veganism as a trick of the trade, so to speak—as both a weight-loss plan and a front so no one will notice you're anorexic. When Georgia Hollenbeck,

For people with an eating disorder, being vegetarian or vegan can provide a convenient excuse to avoid eating, since many foods contain animal products.

24, was in her early teens and spiraling into anorexia and bulimia, the veterinary worker decided to give veganism a try after reading about it on one of these sites. "I'm from Michigan, so we eat a lot of meat here," she said. As such, becoming vegan allowed her to say "no, thanks" to meals much of the time, and allowed her eating disorders to flourish in secret.

Of course, some embark on vegan diets for all the seemingly right reasons, only to find themselves on a slippery slope to disordered eating. As with alcohol or cigarettes, exposure combined with biological predisposition can lead to abuse. "Going on any kind of diet where you're paying a lot of attention to what you eat or don't eat puts you at risk for an eating disorder," says Herrin. "Especially when you label certain foods as 'bad.'"

Orthorexia

Recently, reports of "orthorexia" have captured headlines. Those who suffer from the controversial new disorder compulsively avoid foods thought to be unhealthy or unnatural, including products with trans fats, artificial colors, or flavors, high-fructose corn syrup, and preservatives. Often, orthorexics opt for a strict vegan diet. Some say orthorexia represents this dangerous slide from health to pathology.

To ensure both physical and psychological health, emerging vegans should educate themselves on how to maintain balanced nutrition and weight, says Keri Gans, a spokesman for the American Dietetic Association and a practicing dietician in Manhattan. Replacing meat and dairy with plant-based sources of protein and fat is crucial, as is taking certain vitamin supplements. If they're not vigilant, vegans can become lethargic and malnourished; they're particularly at risk for Vitamin B-12 deficiency, which can lead to deterioration of the spinal cord.

"A person who undertakes veganism as a lifestyle, not related to any kind of eating disorder, will know that they have to replace the foods they've eliminated with new foods," says Gans. "If they're saying to me, 'Let's talk about ways to add more foods into my diet, I'm not afraid of healthy fats,' I'll say to myself, 'OK, this person gets it.'" If not, the veganism may be a red flag.

Compassionate Self-Care

Perhaps counterintuitively, some who are in recovery from an eating disorder say adopting a vegan diet helped to nurse them back to health. After struggling with anorexia and drug use in her 20s, Mandi Babkes embarked on an all-raw, vegan diet. She now runs a holistic health practice and raw-food vegan catering business in Pittsburgh, explaining that while her eating disorders were about self-destruction, her veganism is about self-love. "Being a vegan and raw foodist really helped me to feel better, to feel cleaner, to feel more energized," she said. "I sleep better, and I have a brighter outlook."

Still, many dieticians and eating-disorder specialists hesitate to recommend a vegan diet as a path to recovery. "It's like an alcoholic who likes to spend time in bars," says Herrin. "It's very risky to take on any system of eating that's restrictive and passes judgment on food that's not founded on health principles."

Perhaps above all, clinicians and vegan advocates alike emphasize one underlying message: At its most basic level, veganism is about practicing non-violence toward animals. And in keeping with this philosophy, its followers should look out for their own well-being, too.

ELEVEN

The Experience of Being Vegan and Vegetarian in High School

Brittany Estes-Garcia

Brittany Estes-Garcia is a young writer who has been vegetarian her entire life and recently became a vegan. In the following selection Estes-Garcia discusses her experience of being vegan in high school, as well as relating stories of other high school vegetarians. For example, Binni, whose Hindu family raised her as a vegetarian, was fully supported in her choice and was able to simply bring food from home. In contrast, Veronica's Mexican household strongly opposed her vegetarianism and required her to keep eating some meat for years after she had made the decision to become vegetarian. Eventually her family decided to support her lifestyle choice. Other issues discussed are the impulse to try to convert others to a vegetarian lifestyle and the challenge of staying true to one's beliefs in the face of opposition.

Out of personal experience, it is evident to me that veganism and vegetarianism are on the rise, especially with teenagers and in high schools. Some teenagers choose this route because they want to support the environment through their food choices, or simply because it is "in" or "trendy." Others are attracted to it for health reasons. Along with different reasons, everyone has different experiences being vegan or vegetarian as well. Some teenagers receive support from the people that surround them and others don't. Some teenagers have no problems finding vegan or vegetarian options for food, while others struggle. Some teenagers were vegan or vegetarian before high school and continued their diet; others have to adjust to a completely new lifestyle. So what is it really like to be a vegan or vegetarian in high school? As a life-long vegetarian, I have one perspective. For this article, I contacted other vegetarian teens.

Binni, a Hindu girl, is vegetarian for religious reasons but says, "I would have been vegetarian anyway." She has been vegetarian her whole life and because of this hasn't had to struggle with adjusting to a new lifestyle or trying to remember to get foods that don't have meat when she's standing in the cafeteria line at school. In fact, she said, "I just bring food from home." Her family and friends have all supported her because it is part of their lifestyle as well.

An Abundance of Vegetarian Choices

One of the questions that vegan and vegetarian teenagers are asked most often is how hard is it to find food. When asked about the contents of her meals, Binni said this, "Breakfast is usually just some orange juice and fruit. Lunch and dinner are usually granola bars, water, fruit, salads, and Indian foods." Some of her favorite Indian food dishes are roti, samosa, papads, khichdi, and dosa. Roti is a flatbread and the simplest recipe involves only flour, water, and butter, for which vegans can substitute margarine. Samosas are pastry snacks that are usually filled with vegetables. Papads, which are often called pappadum, are crispy wafers that can be dipped in sauce or served with other foods. Khichdi is a rice dish that has different vegetables and spices. Dosas are spicy, thin crepes, stuffed with filling, such as a potato mixture.

Another girl named Veronica had an experience that is the complete opposite from Binni's. She grew up in a Mexican house-

Teenagers at some schools have no problem finding vegan or vegetarian food options such as this at school while others struggle with a lack of choices at their schools.

hold that was strongly against the idea of her becoming a vegetarian, and attended a Future Farmers of America high school that raised various animals to be sold off to slaughterhouses. Unlike Binni, she didn't receive support from anyone until her parents became very supportive in her freshman year of high school. Before then, her parents made her continue to eat some meats, mainly chicken and seafood. What made her become vegetarian when so many people who didn't agree with her views surrounded her? She described it like this. "I remember being in about first grade and finding out that the chicken nuggets in my Happy Meal came from the same animal roaming around my uncle's house. I had never connected the fact that what I was dipping in my ketchup was once alive! As soon as I figured that out, I refused to eat meat."

Vegetarian Youth in the United States

In an online poll of people aged eight to eighteen conducted by Harris Interactive on behalf of the Vegetarian Resource Group, participants were asked, "Please tell us which of the following foods, if any, do you never eat: I never eat . . . Meat; Poultry; Fish/Seafood; Dairy Products; Eggs; Honey; I eat all these foods."

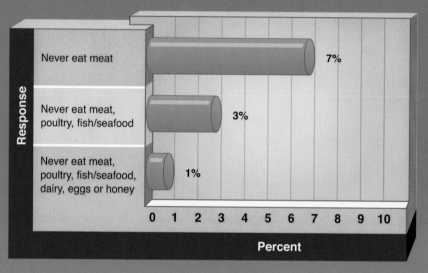

Taken from: Charles Stahler. "How Many Youth Are Vegetarian?" Vegetarian Resource Group, February 24, 2010. www.vrg.org/press/youth–poll_2010.php.

As for food she described finding vegetarian food as simply being "less convenient." She would pack her lunch or eat the sides or other options that were available to her at school like pastas. In her lunch, she would make sandwiches and wraps with meat substitutes like fake turkey and ham. When she got old enough to drive to lunch from school, she said, "It was very easy finding places to eat." Many restaurants would replace animal products with other items in her meals such as tofu or more vegetables. For example, [Italian-restaurant chain] Johnny Carino's would usually replace meat with cheese or eggplant; [Chinese-takeout chain] Pei Wei would substitute tofu; and a restaurant called MeKong would substitute tofu as would several sushi restaurants. A lot of restaurants also had veggie burgers. During her last year of high school she volunteered with senior citizens during lunch and the chef there would sometimes make vegetarian meals for her. Now, she eats cereal with vegan milks such as soymilk, almond milk, or rice milk along with fruits and bagels for breakfast. She also eats vegetarian Morningstar sausage links or patties. For lunch, she eats veggie burgers, falafel wraps, eggplant pastas, pitas, rice, and tofu when she is away at college. She also eats at Taco Bell where they will replace meat with beans, or Kashi frozen dinners. If she is home she will eat stir-fried vegetables, including mushrooms, red peppers, and broccoli, along with Whole Foods' vegan shrimp. She also recommends Morningstar fake meats for lunch. As for dinner, she usually eats the vegetarian options that are on campus, or pastas, veggie burgers from Chili's, or veggie sandwiches from McCallister's [deli chain]. Although her diet has changed since high school because she has had to adjust to a college lifestyle, these are still good suggestions for high school vegans or vegetarians to eat.

Teasing and Family Opposition

My story fits nicely in the middle. I was born and raised as a vegetarian and recently made the switch to become vegan around a year ago. My mother raised me this way for moral reasons. She said she would never eat "anything that has eyes" and that vegetarianism is healthier for the planet and us. While my mother is very supportive and is the one that introduced me to this lifestyle, my other family members and often my peers have not been as accepting. My dad does not share our views, which makes it complicated. My families on both sides often call my mother and me "tree-huggers" and look at us funny when we eat Tofurky on Thanksgiving, but I don't let it get me down. I also have gone to a high school that is open towards vegetarians and vegans, and have met quite a few vegetarians from my time there. I am now a distance learner and while socialization is not traditional, I have still "met" quite a few people that share my views. If they didn't share my views, they simply wanted to learn more about my diet choices. That does not mean I haven't faced hostility from my peers though. What I remember the most is getting pieces of meat waved around in front of me in elementary school when a boy found out I didn't eat meat.

Food hasn't been hard for me to find. I had gotten used to taking my lunch to school because until high school my school didn't have a cafeteria so that wasn't a problem. For lunch, I would eat vegetables such as cooked broccoli and carrots. I brought a lot of sandwiches and wraps, and would also eat rice cakes with almond butter or peanut butter. My favorite things to bring for lunch were vegan pesto pasta and vegan chocolate chip cookies from Whole Foods. Most restaurants will replace animal products like they did for Veronica, and like Binni, I eat a lot of fruit and vegetables. It helps because my mom shares my lifestyle so she cooks me vegan foods that we eat together.

Overall, food doesn't have to be an issue once it gets easier to figure out how to substitute things, or the right resources are found. There are vegan or vegetarian substitutes for virtually everything, even the eggs in cookies and brownies. These foods are all very tasty and filling as well. There are plenty of resources on the Internet concerning vegan and vegetarian recipes. The Vegetarian Resource Group would be a good start. Books are also very helpful, and can also be read to find out more about vegetarianism and veganism in general. A good cookbook I recommend is called, *Vegan Vittles* and has stories about rescued animals throughout. A book that Veronica recommends is called *Animal Liberation*.

Staying True to One's Beliefs

Another issue that comes up a lot is trying to inform people and get them to try the vegan or vegetarian lifestyle. I have gotten five of my friends to try being vegetarian. Binni said she got someone to be vegetarian once, but as she says," it only lasted a week for them." Veronica, on the other hand, described it like this, "At first I was concerned about converting everyone around me. However, over time, I became more comfortable about making my choice to be a vegetarian for myself. I've become more comfortable with my differences and how radically different my lifestyle seems to be at times." As a vegan or vegetarian in high school, it is hard not to want to try to make other people see what is happening with the animals in the world. A good option is to get involved with organizations that share similar views. For example, Veronica worked with the Humane Society and is going to intern with The Vegetarian Resource Group, including writing articles for the *Vegetarian Journal*. I am writing articles for the Vegetarian Resource Group, like this one, and also volunteer with PETA [People for the Ethical Treatment of Animals] and write for an organization called Compassion Over Killing.

Becoming vegan or vegetarian in high school or continuing to be a vegan or vegetarian in high school is an important decision in one's life. Veronica had some advice, "I became a vegetarian for the ethical reasons behind that diet. If it wasn't for the compassion I feel for animals, I would not be able to distinguish what I put on my plate. Never get discouraged. The media reporting the 3,934,949 cases of animal abuse a year should not keep you from doing what you think is right. Nor should the people around you who are drooling while waiting for those ribs to be ready. Nor should the new 'trendy' leather or fur accessories. Choosing to be vegan is an enlightening decision that should not be affected by discouragement." Binni had some advice as well, saying, "Do it! It's a more natural and healthier lifestyle choice and you feel better about your body and soul. It's just the way it's supposed to be." As for me, I would like to say that becoming a vegan makes you feel healthier, and like you are making a good impact on the world just by changing your diet. It is completely worth it.

What You Should Know About Vegetarianism

Facts About Vegetarianism

According to the Vegetarianism in America study, published by *Vegetarian Times* in 2008,

- 3.2 percent of the US adult population (7.3 million people) practice a vegetarian diet;
- 0.5 percent (1 million adults) are vegan (eliminate all animal products from their diet);
- 10 percent (22.8 million people) practice a "vegetarian-inclined" diet (sometimes called "flexitarian" or "semi-vegetarian");
- 5.2 percent (11.9 million) indicated an interest in practicing a vegetarian diet at some point in the future;

Motivations cited for adopting a vegetarian diet break down as follows (more than one might apply):

- health improvement (53 percent)
- environmental concerns (47 percent)
- "natural approaches to wellness" (39 percent)
- concerns with food safety (31 percent)
- concern for animal welfare (54 percent)
- weight loss (25 percent)
- weight maintenance (24 percent)

The Vegetarian Resource Group reported in May 2012 the following:

- The frequency with which people in the United States eat vegetarian meals:

- 7 percent eat one vegetarian meal per week;
- 7 percent eat vegetarian one day per week;
- 15 percent eat many vegetarian meals per week but fewer than half of all meals;
- 14 percent eat vegetarian for more than half of all meals; and
- 4 percent always eat vegetarian meals;
- Respondents who indicated that they never eat meat, fish, or poultry included:
  - 5 percent of females
  - 3 percent of males
  - 3 percent of whites
  - 6 percent of blacks
  - 8 percent of Hispanics

According to a 2010 national poll by the VRG, of US youth 18 years of age or younger:

- 7 percent never eat meat (but eat fish or poultry)
- 8 percent of males never eat meat
- 7 percent of females never eat meat
- 8 percent of those aged 8–12 never eat meat
- 7 percent of those aged 13–18 never eat meat
- 12 percent of males aged 10–12 never eat meat
- 3 percent of females aged 10–12 never eat meat
- 5 percent of males aged 13–15 never eat meat
- 9 percent of females aged 13–15 never eat meat
- 22 percent under 18 never eat fish
- 7 percent never eat poultry
- 11 percent never eat eggs
- 6 percent never dairy products
- 21 percent never eat honey

The VRG estimates that about 1.4 million US youth under 18 are vegetarian, and about 3 million never eat meat.

Consumer market research firm Mintel reported in June 2013 that
- in 2012, $553 million worth of meat alternatives were sold in the United States, up 8 percent from 2010; and

- although only 7 percent of food consumers think of themselves as vegetarian, 36 percent of those surveyed use meat alternatives.

Environmental and Health Considerations of Meat Consumption Versus Vegetarianism

According to a study by researchers at Loma Linda University published in 2012:

- Vegetarian Seventh-day Adventist women in California live an average of 85.7 years, compared to 79.6 years for nonvegetarian California women.
- Vegetarian Adventist men live an average of 83.3 years, compared to 73.8 years for nonvegetarian California men.
- On average, vegans weigh thirty pounds less than those who eat meat.

According to "Eating Animals: 10 Reasons to Avoid Factory Farmed Flesh," published in *Sojourners* magazine in May 2010:

- On average, those living in the United States consume the equivalent of twenty-one thousand animals during their lifetimes.
- Most of those animals are from factory farms, which account for 99 percent of turkeys, 97 percent of egg-laying hens, 99.9 percent of chickens raised for meat, 95 percent of pigs, and 78 percent of cattle.
- US farm animals create 130 times as much waste by volume as do humans, amounting to about 43.5 tons of feces per second. Virtually no waste-treatment facilities for farm animals exist.

According to *Livestock's Long Shadow*, a report published by the Food and Agriculture Organization (FAO) of the United Nations in 2006:

- Seventy percent of all agricultural land on earth, and 30 percent of the total land mass, is used to raise animals for food;
- 18 percent of climate-changing greenhouse gas emissions come from the livestock industry; more than that from transportation;

- in the United States, food animals account for about 55 percent of soil erosion, 37 percent of pesticide use, 50 percent of antibiotics, and 33.3 percent of the phosphorus and nitrogen contaminating freshwater resources;
- 20 percent of the biomass of all animals on the planet is accounted for by animals raised for food (as opposed to wild animals); and
- 30 percent of land that was once home to wildlife is now used by livestock.

Kathy Freston, drawing from various sources, reported the following in a *Huffington Post* article in April 2009:
- If everyone in the United States ate vegetarian food for one day, altogether the country would save:
  - 100 billion gallons of water,
  - 1.5 billion pounds of crops that would have been fed to meat animals,
  - 70 million gallons of gas,
  - 3 million acres of agricultural land,
  - 33 tons of antibiotics,
  - greenhouse gas emissions equal to about 1.2 million tons of carbon dioxide,
  - 3 million tons of soil erosion,
  - 4.5 million tons of animal feces, and
  - 7 tons of ammonia pollution.
- If everyone in the United States ate vegetarian food instead of chicken one day per week, the reduction in carbon dioxide emissions would be equal to eliminating five hundred thousand cars.
- Around the world, 756 million tons of grain are fed to animals raised for food. If that grain were fed to the 1.4 billion underfed people in the world, each would receive more than 3 pounds of grain per day—twice the amount needed to survive.

Pasture-Raised Animals

The group Eat Wild, compiling data from various sources, reports the following facts:
- Meat from animals fed on a diet of grass has less fat and fewer calories than meat from an animal fed grain; e.g., a 6-ounce

steak from a grass-fed steer may have 100 fewer calories than an equivalent steak from a steer fed grain. Someone with average beef consumption (66.5 pounds/year) who switched to lean, grass-fed beef would consume 17,733 fewer calories per year.

- Omega-3 fatty acids are a healthy type of fat that is often lacking in the US diet. Grass-fed animals produce meat with two to four times the amount of omega-3 fatty acids of that of animals fed grain.
- Similarly, eggs from pastured hens may have up to ten times the amount of omega-3s of factory-raised hens.
- Much less fossil fuel is required to produce meat from animals fed grass than to produce grain-fed animals; for every two calories of energy from the meat of grass-fed animals, only one calorie of fossil-fuel energy was used; conversely, five to ten calories of fossil fuel are required for each calorie of food in meat from a grain-fed animal.
- In comparing Minnesota ranches that raised animals on pasture to nearby farms that grew soybeans, oats, hay, or corn, researchers found that the pastured land had 131 percent more earthworms and 53 percent more soil stability (i.e., resistance to erosion).
- Carbon sequestration is a process in which plants remove the carbon dioxide from the air and store it in the soil as carbon, which helps reduce the threat of climate change. Soils on grazing land (which are covered with wild grasses) were found to store more than forty tons of carbon per acre, compared with twenty-six tons per acre for land used to grow food crops.
- A cow raised in a factory farm tends to live only two to three years; in contrast, those raised on pasture can live up to twelve years.
- Three billion tons of topsoil are lost in the United States each year; much of this is due to conventional methods for raising livestock; in contrast, pasture-raised animals cause up to 93 percent less topsoil loss.

What You Should Do About Vegetarianism

Gather Information

The first step in grappling with any complex and controversial issue is to be informed about it. Gather as much information as you can from a variety of sources. The essays in this book form an excellent starting point, representing a variety of viewpoints and approaches to the topic. Your school or local library will be another source of useful information; look there for relevant books, magazines, and encyclopedia entries. The bibliography and Organizations to Contact sections of this book will give you useful starting points in gathering additional information.

The last several decades have seen an enormous increase in the amount of information available on vegetarianism and related dietary matters. Many scientific articles and reports on all aspects of the topic have been published. If the information in such articles is too dense or technical, check the abstract at the beginning of the article, which provides a clear summary of the research's conclusions.

Internet search engines will be helpful to you in your search. There are many blogs and websites that cover vegetarianism and other diets from a variety of perspectives, including concerned individuals offering their opinions and advice, advocacy organizations, popular media outlets, and governmental and scientific organizations. (See **Evaluate Your Information Sources,** below, on this, however.)

Identify the Issues Involved

Once you have gathered your information, review it methodically to discover the key issues involved. Why do some people choose a vegetarian diet? What benefits does such a diet have in terms of health, the environment, ethics, animal rights, or other considerations? Are there any downsides or dangers associated with a vegetarian diet? What are some of the criticisms people make of vegetarianism? What different types of vegetarian diet exist? Why do people choose one type of vegetarianism over another? What are the best ways to promote a vegetarian or other personal dietary choice?

Evaluate Your Information Sources

In developing your own opinion, it is vital to evaluate the sources of the information you have discovered. Authors of books, magazine articles, and so forth, however well intentioned, have their own perspectives and biases that may affect how they present information and draw conclusions on the subject. In some cases people and organizations may deliberately distort information to support a strongly held ideological or moral stance—signs of this include oversimplification and extreme positions.

Consider the authors' credentials and organizational affiliations. Authors may offer information that is perfectly valid but favor data that support their viewpoints and those of the organizations they are associated with. For example, a representative of a vegan/strict vegetarian organization might see any use of animals in agriculture as unacceptable under any circumstances and only mention negative consequences associated with the meat industry, such as the suffering of animals in factory farms. Conversely, someone working for the cattle industry may present consumption of meat as an essential aspect of US culture or cite only reports portraying vegetarianism in a negative light.

On the other hand, if you find someone arguing against his or her expected bias—such as a vegan arguing in favor of the use of animals in agriculture in some circumstances, or a meat eater advocating less consumption of meat—it may be worthwhile to pay particular attention to what he or she is saying. Always critically evaluate and assess your sources rather than take whatever they say at face value.

Examine Your Own Perspective

Consider your own beliefs, feelings, and biases on this subject. Perhaps you have been influenced by the attitudes of family or friends, or media reports. If you had a position on vegetarianism before reading this book, consider what it might take to change your mind. Seek out and contemplate information and perspectives that differ from what you already believe to be true. Be aware of "confirmation bias," the tendency to look for evidence that confirms what you already believe to be true and to discount anything that contradicts your viewpoint. In the case of vegetarianism, try it out for yourself so you can argue from experience as well as from ideas.

Form Your Own Opinion and Take Action

Once you have gathered and organized information, identified the issues involved, examined your own perspective, and garnered your own experience, you will be ready to form an opinion on vegetarianism and to advocate your position in debates and discussions. If you decide to become a vegetarian, you will have a better idea of how to do so in a healthy way. Perhaps you have not yet made up your mind on the subject. If that is the case, ask yourself what you would need to know to make up your mind; perhaps a bit more research would be helpful. Whatever position you take, be prepared to explain it clearly based on facts, evidence, and well-thought-out opinions.

There are many things you can do about vegetarianism or dietary concerns in general. An easy action is simply to talk with people around you about food and where it comes from. If you are doing a school report on the subject, do it on something meaningful to you, such as raw foods, environmental considerations of different farming methods, or the value of meat in a diet. You could write an editorial for your school paper or a local paper, or a blog entry, advocating your beliefs. If the school cafeteria does not offer food choices you want or need, you could lobby the school administration about it or talk to the principal or Parent-Teacher Association. You could ask the managers at local supermarkets to stock the types of food (e.g., grass-fed beef or particular vegetarian foods) that you want to find in their stores. You can ask your parents whether you can eat meat or not eat meat one day a week to see how you feel.

Another great way to support your beliefs is by volunteering. If animal welfare is something that concerns you, you may wish to contact an organization such as Farm Animal Rights Movement and ask what you can do to help. Or you might help work a booth at a farmers' market or work on a local farm. The ways you can help put your beliefs into action in the world are only limited by your imagination.

The editors have compiled the following list of organizations concerned with the issues debated in this book. The descriptions are derived from materials provided by the organizations. All have publications or information available for interested readers. The list was compiled on the date of publication of the present volume; names, addresses, phone and fax numbers, and e-mail and Internet addresses may change. Be aware that many organizations take several weeks or longer to respond to inquiries, so allow as much time as possible.

American Vegan Society (AVS)
56 Dinshah Ln., PO Box 369
Malaga, NJ 08328
(856) 694-2887
fax: (856) 694-2288
website: www.americanvegan.org

AVS is a nonprofit educational membership organization teaching a compassionate way of living that includes veganism. AVS publishes the magazine *American Vegan*, which is available by subscription. Its website offers information on veganism, a free online newsletter, and links to additional vegan-related information and resources.

Center for Science in the Public Interest (CSPI)
1220 L St. NW, Ste. 300
Washington, DC 20005
(202) 332-9110
fax: (202) 265-4954
website: www.cspinet.org

CSPI is an advocate for nutrition and health, food safety, alcohol policy, and sound science. Founded by executive director Michael Jacobson and two other scientists, CSPI seeks to educate the public, advocate government policies that are consistent with scientific evidence on health and environmental issues, and counter industry's powerful influence on public opinion and public policies. CSPI publishes an award-winning newsletter, *Nutrition Action Healthletter*, and its website contains food and nutrition news and other information, including articles about the value of plant-based diets.

Compassionate Cooks
PO Box 16104
Oakland, CA 94610
e-mail: info@compassionatecooks.com
website: www.compassionatecooks.com

Compassionate Cooks is the website of Colleen Patrick-Goudreau, author of several books on veganism, including *On Being Vegan: Reflections on a Compassionate Life* and *The 30-Day Vegan Challenge: The Ultimate Guide to Eating Cleaner, Getting Leaner, and Living Compassionately*. The Compassionate Cooks website features the Food for Thought podcast, videos, recipes, a free newsletter, and links to resources of interest to people practicing or exploring veganism.

Compassion Over Killing (COK)
PO Box 9773
Washington, DC 20016
(301) 891-2458
e-mail: info@cok.net
website: www.cok.net

COK is a national nonprofit animal advocacy organization headquartered in Washington, D.C., with an additional office in Los Angeles, California. Working to end animal abuse since 1995, COK focuses on cruelty to animals in agriculture and promotes vegetarian eating as a way to build a kinder world for both humans and other animals. Its website features reports on undercover investigations into animal cruelty in agribusiness, a blog, an e-newsletter, a free "Vegetarian Starter Guide," and links to vegetarian and animal rights news.

Eat Wild
PO Box 7321
Tacoma, WA 98417
(866) 453-8489
fax: (253) 759-2318
e-mail: info2011@eatwild.com
website: www.eatwild.com

Eat Wild provides a website dedicated to research-based information about choosing present-day foods that approach the nutritional content of wild plants and game, which the organization believes provide superior nutrition to the modern diet. Its website provides information on food safety, ways in which pasture-based farming enhances animal welfare and benefits the health of consumers and the environment, and links to relevant resources, including local suppliers of grass-fed products.

Farm Animal Rights Movement (FARM)
10101 Ashburton Ln.
Bethesda, MD 20817
(888) 327-6872
e-mail: info@farmusa.org
website: www.farmusa.org

FARM is a national public-interest organization that promotes plant-based (vegan) diets to save animals, reduce global warming, conserve environmental resources, and improve public health. The group publishes an e-newsletter and its website provides information about vegetarianism, including a section on the environmental, health, animal rights, and other benefits of a vegetarian diet.

International Vegetarian Union of North America (IVU North America)
c/o Vegetarian Society of DC
PO Box 4921
Washington, DC 20008
e-mail: vuna@ivu.org
website: www.ivu.org

IVU North America is a network of vegetarian groups throughout the United States and Canada. Membership is open only to groups, but individuals can be supporters. As an independent regional organization of the International Vegetarian Union, IVU North America serves as a liaison with the worldwide vegetarian movement and seeks to promote a strong, effective, and cooperative vegetarian movement throughout North America. The IVU North America website provides news, vegetarian recipes, and instructions for starting local vegetarian groups.

National Cattlemen's Beef Association
9110 E. Nichols Ave. #300
Centennial, CO 80112
(303) 694-0305
e-mail: cattle@beef.org
website: www.beef.org

The National Cattlemen's Beef Association is the marketing organization and trade association for America's 1 million cattle farmers and ranchers. The group promotes beef consumption, and its website contains a section on beef production that addresses such issues as the environment, animal welfare, and nutrition.

North American Vegetarian Society (NAVS)
PO Box 72
Dolgeville, NY 13329
(518) 588-7970
e-mail: navs@telenet.net
website: www.navs-online.org

NAVS is a nonprofit, tax-exempt educational organization founded in 1974. Its twofold mission is (1) to provide a support network for members, affiliated groups, and vegetarians in general; and (2) to inform the public about how vegetarianism benefits humans, other animals, and the earth. NAVS publishes the quarterly magazine *Vegetarian Voice*, advises the media, and assists individuals with inquiries. The organization's website includes a free e-newsletter, answers to frequently asked questions (FAQ) about vegetarianism, recipes, and other information useful to those curious about or practicing a vegetarian lifestyle.

People for the Ethical Treatment of Animals (PETA)
501 Front St.
Norfolk, VA 23510
(757) 622-7382
fax: (757) 622-0457
e-mail: info@peta.org
website: www.peta.org

PETA is a controversial animal rights and advocacy organization that focuses its attention on four areas of animal suffering: factory farms, laboratories, the clothing trade, and the entertainment industry. The group also works on a variety of other issues, including the cruel killing of beavers, birds, and other "pests," and the abuse of backyard dogs. PETA provides public education; conducts cruelty investigations, research, and animal rescue; promotes legislation; and sponsors special events, celebrity involvement, and protest campaigns. The PETA website offers information about animal rights, factory farms, and other reasons for adopting a vegetarian diet.

Sustainable Table
c/o GRACE Communications Foundation
215 Lexington Ave.
New York, NY 10016
(212) 726-9161
e-mail: info@sustainabletable.org
website: www.sustainabletable.org

Sustainable Table was established in 2003 to promote sustainable food and to educate consumers about food-related issues. The organization produced a popular video called *The Meatrix*, which (along with two sequel videos) humorously educates consumers about the problems caused by factory farms. Sustainable Table also offers an Eat Well Guide that lists over twenty-five thousand sustainable food resources in the United States and Canada, as well as the blog *Ecocentric*, which covers food, water, and energy issues. Its website also includes a podcast and links to videos on sustainability.

Vegetarian Resource Group (VRG)
PO Box 1463
Baltimore, MD 21203
(410) 366-8343
fax: (410) 366-8804
e-mail: vrg@vrg.org
website: www.vrg.org

VRG is a nonprofit organization dedicated to educating the public on vegetarianism and interrelated issues of health, nutrition, ecology, ethics, and world hunger. In addition to publishing a quarterly magazine, the *Vegetarian Journal* (back issues of which can be read online for free), VRG produces and sells cookbooks, other books, pamphlets, and article reprints. The VRG website is a good source of information about vegetarian nutrition and recipes and offers a free e-newsletter. Of particular interest is the section "Vegetarian Kids, Teens, and Family," which includes videos, an essay contest, and information on VRG's five-thousand-dollar college scholarship for vegetarian high school students.

Vegetarian Society of the United Kingdom
Parkdale, Dunham Rd.
Altrincham, Chesire WA14 4QG, UK
+44 (0)161 925 2000
fax: +44 (0)161 926 9182
e-mail: info@vegsoc.org
website: www.vegsoc.org

The Vegetarian Society of the United Kingdom is an educational charity promoting understanding and respect for vegetarian lifestyles. It offers advice about nutritional issues, environmental impact, and other aspects of vegetarianism. The group's website contains a wealth of information about vegetarianism—everything from statistics and information sheets on factory farming techniques to recipes and restaurant guides.

BIBLIOGRAPHY

Books

Claire Askew, *Generation V: The Complete Guide to Going, Being, and Staying Vegan as a Teenager*. Oakland, CA: PM, 2011.

Mark Bittman, *Food Matters: A Guide to Conscious Eating with More than 75 Recipes*. New York: Simon & Schuster, 2009.

Tovar Cerulli, *The Mindful Carnivore: A Vegetarian's Hunt for Sustenance*. New York: Pegasus, 2012.

Kathy Freston, *Veganist: Lose Weight, Get Healthy, Change the World*. New York: Weinstein, 2011.

Catherine Friend, *The Compassionate Carnivore; Or, How to Keep Animals Happy, Save Old MacDonald's Farm, Reduce Your Hoofprint, and Still Eat Meat*. Cambridge, MA: Da Capo Lifelong, 2008.

Alexandra Greeley, *The Everything Guide to Being Vegetarian: The Advice, Nutrition Information, and Recipes You Need to Enjoy a Healthy Lifestyle*. Avon, MA: Adams Media, 2009.

Victoria Moran and Adair Moran, *Main Street Vegan: Everything You Need to Know to Eat Healthfully and Live Compassionately in the Real World*. New York: Tarcher/Penguin, 2012.

Margaret Pasewicz, *Cultural Encyclopedia of Vegetarianism*. Santa Barbara, CA: Greenwood, 2010.

Colleen Patrick-Goudreau, *The 30-Day Vegan Challenge: The Ultimate Guide to Eating Cleaner, Getting Leaner, and Living Compassionately*. New York: Ballantine, 2011.

Reuben Proctor and Lars Thomsen, *Veganissimo A to Z: A Comprehensive Guide to Identifying and Avoiding Ingredients of Animal Origin in Everyday Products*. New York: Experiment, 2012.

John Robbins, *No Happy Cows: Dispatches from the Frontlines of the Food Revolution*. San Francisco: Conari, 2012.

Jo Robinson, *Eating on the Wild Side: The Missing Link to Optimum Health*. New York: Little, Brown, 2013.

Rod Rotondi, *Raw Food for Real People: Living Vegan Food Made Simple by the Chef and Founder of Leaf Organics*. Novato, CA: New World Library, 2009.

Ellen L. Shanley and Colleen A. Thompson, *Fueling the Teen Machine: What It Takes to Make Good Choices for Yourself Every Day*. Palo Alto, CA: Bull, 2011.

Arran Stephens and Eliot Jay Rosen, *The Compassionate Diet: How What You Eat Can Change Your Life and Save the Planet*. Emmaus, PA: Rodale, 2011.

Gene Stone, ed., *Forks Over Knives: The Plant-Based Way to Strength*. New York: Experiment, 2011.

Susan M. Traugh, *Vegetarianism*. Detroit: Lucent, 2011.

Tara Austen Weaver, *The Butcher and the Vegetarian: One Woman's Romp Through a World of Men, Meat, and Moral Crisis*. Emmaus, PA: Rodale, 2010.

Periodicals & Internet Sources

Marc Abrahams, "Mincing Vegetarians Rather than Words: Researchers Have Tried to Show Why Vegetarianism Provokes Hostility," *The Guardian* (Manchester, UK), July 2, 2012.

Keith Akers, "Are Humans Naturally Vegetarian?," Compassionate Spirit, April 21, 2012. www.compassionatespirit.com.

Mike Archer, "Ordering the Vegetarian Meal? There's More Animal Blood on Your Hands," The Conversation, December 16, 2011. http://theconversation.com.

Matt Ball, "Belief on the Right Side of History," Vegan Outreach. www.veganoutreach.org.

Susie Cagle, "Ticks Are Turning Victims into Vegetarians," Grist, November 9, 2012. http://grist.org.

Tovar Cerulli, "Devouring the World: A Former Vegan Who Now Hunts Deer Is Troubled by What It Takes to Put Food on Our Plates," *Aeon Magazine*, September 17, 2012. www.aeonmagazine.com.

Rob Dunn, "Ancient Humans Mostly Vegetarian, 'Paleolithic Diet' Critic Says," *Huffington Post*, July 23, 2012. www.huffingtonpost .com.

Ahmed ElAmin, "Intensive Meat Production a Danger to Food Supply, Warns FAO," Food Navigator USA, September 17, 2007. www.foodnavigator-usa.com.

Simon Fairlie, "Meat Eating vs Vegetarian or Vegan Diets," *Permaculture*, August 31, 2010.

Max Fisher, "The Case for Semitarianism," *Atlantic Monthly*, June 17, 2009.

Kathy Freston, "Why Do Vegetarians Live Longer?," *Huffington Post*, October 26, 2012. www.huffingtonpost.com.

William T. Jarvis, "Why I Am Not a Vegetarian," Quackwatch, June 17, 2006. www.quackwatch.org.

"Junk-Food Vegetarianism: How to Choose Fruits and Veggies Instead of Crackers and Chips," *Living Green Magazine*, June 21, 2013. http://livinggreenmag.com.

Satoshi Kanazawa, "Empathy Is What Really Sets Vegetarians Apart (at Least Neurologically Speaking)," *Psychology Today*, May 31, 2010.

Michele Kayal, "The Fresh, Mainstream Look of Vegetarianism," *Fort Collins Coloradoan*, April 29, 2013.

Barbara J. King, "Want To Help Animals? No Vegan Extremism Required, *Cosmos and Culture* (blog), National Public Radio, March 28, 2013. www.npr.org.

Felicity Lawrence, "Is It Time We Cut Down on Meat?," *The Guardian* (Manchester, UK), September 11, 2011.

Charles Macurdy, "Anti-Vegetarian Argument Misunderstands the Vegetarian Diet," *Vancouver (BC) Observer* (British Columbia), June 20, 2013.

Megan McArdle, "Preach It, Veggie-Man," *Atlantic Monthly*, January 22, 2008.

James McWilliams, "Only When Meat Is Stigmatized Will Factory Farms Stop Thriving," *Atlantic Monthly*, October 24, 2011.

James E. McWilliams, "The Myth of Sustainable Meat," *New York Times*, April 12, 2012.

Sarah Miller, "Pig, Out: What's It Like to Kill Your Hog and Eat It, Too?," Grist, February 12, 2013. http://grist.org.

Colleen Patrick-Goudreau, "Get Away from Animals and Stop Fearing the Veggies," The Compassionate Cook, September 29, 2010. www.compassionatecook.com.

Sujatha Ramakrishna, "Vegetarianism & Mental Health: Plant-Based Happiness," Global Animal, June 18, 2013. www.global animal.org.

Finlo Rohrer, "The Rise of the Non-Veggie Vegetarian," BBC News, November 5, 2009. http://news.bbc.co.uk.

Olivia Rosewood, "Is Better-ness Good for Anyone?," *Huffington Post*, July 24, 2009. www.huffingtonpost.com.

Peter Singer, "Make Meat-Eaters Pay: Ethicist Proposes Radical Tax, Says They're Killing Themselves and the Planet," *New York Daily News*, October 24, 2009.

Will Tuttle, "Creating a Peaceful World: How Much Does Food Matter?," North American Vegetarian Society. www.navs -online.org.

Shamontiel L. Vaughn, "African Americans Could Fare Well with Vegetarianism," *Chicago Defender*, September 3–9, 2008.

Christopher Wanjek, "Sorry, Vegans: Eating Meat and Cooking Food Is How Humans Got Their Big Brains," *Washington Post*, November 26, 2012.

INDEX

A

Afsari-Mamagani, Grace, 60–62
American Dietetic Association, 15, 21
Amino acids, essential, 16, 29
Anderson, James, 28
Animals
  annual cases of abuse of, 79
  Dalai Lama on killing of, 5–6
  Eating is immoral, 37–42
  emotional lives of, 38
  origins of vegetarianism and, 10–11
  sustainable meat reduces suffering of, 48–52
  vegetarian diet reduces suffering of, 43–47
Animals and Why They Matter (Midgley), 6
Applestone, Joshua, 37

B

Babkes, Mandi, 72
Bekoff, Marc, 37
Blood Type Diet, 33–34
Buddhism, 5, 10–11

C

Calcium, 16, 23
Carlson, Peggy, 5
Carnitine, 23
Centers for Disease Control and Prevention, 32, 33
Cerulli, Tovar, 37
Chissoe, Morgan, 59–60
Christianity, 11
The Compassionate Diet (Stephens and Rosen), 6

D

Da Vinci, Leonardo, 12
D'Adamo, Peter, 33–34
Dalai Lama, 5–6
DDT, 18
Dietary therapy, vegetarianism as, 10
Dietitians of Canada, 15
DMA, 21, 23
Dupler, Douglas, 9

E

Eating disorders
  prevalence of vegetarianism among women with, 69
  veganism is sometimes cover for, 66–72
Einstein, Albert, 12
Emerson, Ralph Waldo, 12
Environment, vegetarianism is good for, 53–57
Epicurus, 11
Estes-Garcia, Brittany, 73

F
Factory farms, 49
Farmers markets, increase in numbers of, 49, 50
Farming, sustainable
  most meat is not produced by, 54–57
  reduces animal suffering, 48–52
FDA (US Food and Drug Administration), 17
Flexitarianism (semi-vegetarianism), 8
Foer, Jonathan Safran, 37–38, 67
Food and Drug Administration, US (FDA), 17
Food pyramid, vegetarian, 14
Food & Wine (magazine), 55–56
Freeman, Aulbry, 63–64
Frey, Rebecca J., 9
Friedman, Danielle, 66

G
Gandhi, Mohandas, 12
Gans, Keri, 71
Grandin, Temple, 51, 51
Greenhouse gases, amounts generated in production of protein, 56
Guarda, Angela, 68

H
Hartnett, Annie, 68

Health concerns
  of meat-based diets, 12–13
  of vegetarian diets, 15–17
Herrin, Marcia, 68, 71, 72
Hinduism, 5, 10
Hollenbeck, Georgia, 70–71
Hymas, Lisa, 53

I
Infants/children, risks of vegetarian diet to, 23–24
Iron, 23
  deficiency of, among women of childbearing age, 32, 33
  dietary sources of, 16

J
Jackson, Shelby, 58
Jainism, 5, 10
Journal of the Academy of Nutrition and Dietetics, 69
Journal of the American Dietetic Association, 68

K
Karan, Donna, 31
Kresser, Chris, 23

L
Lacto-ovo vegetarians, 9–10, 12
  health risks to, 17
Life expectancy
  of feed animals, vs. slaughter age, 45

of vegetarian *vs.* non-vegetarian Seventh-day Adventists, *27*
Lizaola, Veronica, 62

M
Mahabharata (Hindu text), 10
McCartney, Paul, 12
Meat, *32*
  amount produced through sustainable farming, 54–55
  annual per capita consumption of, 17, *35*
  burden on natural resources from production of, 18–19
Meat-based diets
  concerns over health/safety of, 12–13
  plant-based diet is healthier than, 25–29
  vegetarianism is better for environment than, 53–57
Mediterranean diet, 11
Midgley, Mary, 6
Miller, Jill, 66–67

N
Newton, Isaac, 12
Niman, Nicolette Hahn, 37, 41

O
Omega-3 fatty acids, 16, 23
The Omnivore's Dilemma (Pollan), 56
Opinion polls. *See* Surveys

Ornish, Dean, 17
Orthorexia, 71

P
Patrick-Goudreau, Colleen, 43
People for the Ethical Treatment of Animals (PETA), *61*, 70
Pierce, Jessica, 41
Planck, Nina, 20
Plato, 11
Pollan, Michael, 56
Polls. *See* Surveys
Portman, Natalie, 67
Pro-Ana websites, 70
Protein
  carbon dioxide equivalents generated in production of, *56*
  complete, 16
  plant, 29
  soy, *23*
Pythagoras, 11

R
Richichi, Meg, 34
Rosen, Eliot Jay, 6

S
Schaefer, Debbie, 62–63
Schweitzer, Albert, 12
Scott, Dave, 12
Semi-vegetarianism (flexitarianism), 8
Seventh-Day Adventists, 12
  vegetarian *vs.* non-vegetarian, *27*

Shaw, George Bernard, 12
Simpson, Jessica, 69–70
Singer, Isaac Bashevis, 7
Socrates, 11
Soy protein, 23
Spices, health benefits of,
  15
Spirulina, 16
Stephens, Arran, 6
Surveys
  on percentage of people
    identifying themselves as
    vegans, 67
  on prevalence of eating
    disorders among
    vegetarians, 68
  on prevalence of
    vegetarianism among US
    adults, 12
  of women with/without
    eating disorder history, on
    vegetarian status, 69
  of youth, on foods they never
    eat, 76
Sustainable farming
  most meat is not produced
    by, 54–57
  reduces animal suffering
    more than vegetarianism
    does, 48–52

T
Taste, as barrier to dietary
  change, 15
Thoreau, Henry David, 12
Tolstoy, Leo, 12

U
United States, history of
  vegetarianism in, 12–13
Upanishads (Vedic literature),
  10
Uric acid, 26

V
Vegans/veganism, 10
  frequency of Google searches
    for, 39
  is sometimes cover for eating
    disorders, 66–72
  personal account of
    experience of, 73–79
  reasons for choosing, 64
Vegetarian Resource Group,
  12
Vegetarian Society of Great
  Britain, 10
Vegetarianism
  forms of, 9–10
  gentle persuasion wins more
    converts to, 58–65
  is good for environment,
    53–57
  is healthier than meat-based
    diets, 25–29
  is not healthy diet for
    everyone, 30–36
  is not natural for humans,
    20–24
  origins of, 10–12
  prevalence of among women
    with eating disorders, 69

reasons for choosing, 64
sustainable meat reduces
   animal suffering more than,
   48–52
transitioning to, 13–15
Vergara, Hannah, 25
Vitamin B6, 21, 23
Vitamin B12 deficiency, 23,
   71
Vitamins, 16

W
Wild Justice (Bekoff and
   Pierce), 41

Williams, Precious, 30
Woginrich, Jenna, 48
Women
   of childbearing age,
      prevalence of iron
      deficiency among, 32, 33
   with/without eating disorder
      history, 69

Y
Yoga/yogis, 10, *11*

Z
Zinc, 16, 23

© amphotos/Alamy, 32

© AP Images/The Denver Post, John Epperson, 51

© AP Images/Timothy Jacobsen, 55

© Peter Barritt/Alamy, 40

© BSIP SA/Alamy, 70

© Gale, Cengage, 14, 27, 35, 39, 45, 50, 56, 64, 69, 76

© Paul Morigi/Getty Images, 61

© Hagal Nativ/Alamy, 46

© Matthew Sallis/Alamy, 21

© Adrian Sherratt/Alamy, 75

© SuperStock/Alamy, 11

© Peter Titmuss/Alamy, 7

© Janusz Wrobel/Alamy, 28

ISSUES THAT CONCERN YOU

Death and Dying

Lauri S. Scherer, *Book Editor*

GREENHAVEN PRESS
A part of Gale, Cengage Learning

GALE
CENGAGE Learning·

Detroit • New York • San Francisco • New Haven, Conn • Waterville, Maine • London

Elizabeth Des Chenes, *Director, Content Strategy*
Cynthia Sanner, *Publisher*
Douglas Dentino, *Manager, New Product*

For more information, contact:
Greenhaven Press
27500 Drake Rd.
Farmington Hills, MI 48331-3535
Or you can visit our Internet site at gale.cengage.com

For product information and technology assistance, contact us at

Gale Customer Support, 1-800-877-4253
For permission to use material from this text or product, submit all requests online at www.cengage.com/permissions

Further permissions questions can be e-mailed to permissionrequest@cengage.com

Articles in Greenhaven Press anthologies are often edited for length to meet page requirements. In addition, original titles of these works are changed to clearly present the main thesis and to explicitly indicate the author's opinion. Every effort is made to ensure that Greenhaven Press accurately reflects the original intent of the authors. Every effort has been made to trace the owners of copyrighted material.

Cover image © CandyBox Images.

LIBRARY OF CONGRESS CATALOGING-IN-PUBLICATION DATA

Death and dying / Lauri S. Scherer, Book Editor.
    pages cm. -- (Issues that concern you)
Includes bibliographical references and index.
ISBN 978-0-7377-6937-1 (hardcover)
1. Mortality. 2. Death. 3. Terminal care. I. Scherer, Lauri S.
HB1321.D43 2014
362.17'5--dc23
                                      2013037191

Printed in the United States of America
1 2 3 4 5 6 7 18 17 16 15 14

CONTENTS

Introduction   5

1. End-of-Life Care Should Be Minimal and Swift   10
   Ken Murray

2. End-of-Life Care Should Not Necessarily
   Be Minimal and Swift   16
   Cynthia Jones-Nosacek

3. Taking Responsibility for Death   21
   Susan Jacoby

4. Economics Should Not Influence End-of-Life
   Care Decisions   27
   Mike Stopa

5. The Government Should Ration
   End-of-Life Care   33
   M. Gregg Bloche

6. Terminally Ill People Do Not Have the Right to
   Die When and How They Want   40
   Fritz Spencer

7. Legalizing Physician-Assisted Suicide Will
   Lead to Abuse and Coerced Death   45
   Seán P. O'Malley

8. Legalized Physician-Assisted Suicide Has Many
   Safeguards to Prevent Abuse and Coerced Death   52
   Marcia Angell

9. Hospice Care Is Preferable to Assisted Suicide   57
   Linda Campanella

10. **Hospice Care Is Not Preferable to Assisted Suicide**   62
    John M. Crisp

11. **It Is Never Moral to End the Lives of Children**   67
    Andrew Brown

12. **Technology May Allow Humans to Live Forever**   72
    Ray Kurzweil, as told to Duncan Begg

Appendix

    What You Should Know About Death and Dying   76
    What You Should Do About Death and Dying   83

Organizations to Contact   87

Bibliography   94

Index   101

Picture Credits   104

Death and dying are among life's most sensitive, scary, and personal issues. As in life, there are numerous ways to die—suddenly, slowly, in pain, or at peace. Most people hope they will die a "good death," which is universally understood to be a quick, painless exit from the world, free from prolonged suffering, high cost, and great sadness for both the dying and his or her loved ones.

Of course, not all deaths take such form. More often, people suffer from illness or trauma for months or even years. Never quite knowing when disease cannot be beaten, patients, their families, and their physicians must guess at which procedures and interventions to attempt, which ones to forgo, and, most tricky of all, how to know when treatment is no longer worth pursuing.

To help manage end-of-life care and the issues surrounding it, different countries have adopted systematized frameworks to better manage death and dying. Attempts to make death a more comfortable, easy process for the dying and their loved ones have resulted in various medical "protocols," or procedures, for end-of-life care. In the United Kingdom (UK), for example, up until 2014, many hospitals abided by a death-and-dying protocol known as the Liverpool Care Pathway for the Dying Patient (LCP). This set of end-of-life guidelines was originally developed in the late 1990s with the goal of helping hospitals give their dying patients the same high-quality palliative care that terminal patients get in a hospice facility.

Unlike hospice care, in which patients are given the space and time to die more slowly, comfortably, and naturally, hospital care is usually intended for acute, shorter-term care, and is also driven by the Hippocratic oath, by which doctors pledge to "do no harm." As a result, the death-allowing measures (such as withholding food or water) undertaken in hospice settings are typically not pursued in hospitals. "The Hippocratic oath just drives clinicians toward constantly treating the patient, right until the moment they die," explains Sir Thomas Hughes-Hallett, one of the architects of the LCP. He and other supporters of the protocol believe that palliative care offers a dying person the chance to be as comfortable and human as possible, all while letting nature take its course. "It's not about hastening death," he says. "It's about recognizing that someone is dying, and giving them choices. Do you want an oxygen mask over your face? Or would you like to kiss your wife?"[1]

Since its inception, about 130,000 patients have been placed on the LCP each year. They are usually heavily sedated and not given food, water, or other life-sustaining care until they die. "Used correctly, the LCP allows people to die with dignity—surrounded by loved ones rather than machines and in peace, rather than in the violent throes of CPR [cardiopulmonary resuscitation],"[2] writes Manchester, UK, *Guardian* reporter Elizabeth Dzeng. Among doctors especially, the LCP is very popular. In a poll of more than three thousand British doctors, 91 percent said they thought the LCP represented the best care for someone facing death and that it helped people die with dignity. In addition, 90 percent of doctors said they would want to be put on that course of care if they themselves were dying.

Critics of the protocol, however, say it is too easily subject to abuse. They argue that withholding food and water is antithetical to medical care and fear that a patient's wishes may be overlooked by an institution's need to follow procedure. In fact, over time, stories embodying these fears began to emerge in the British media. One such case was Robert Goold, who in February 2013 was brought to a critical-care unit after he sustained a bad fall that caused bleeding in his brain and other serious problems. He was placed on the Liverpool Care Pathway, which withheld food, water, and oxygen in order to allow death to occur naturally. His family claims, however, that they never gave consent for this path of treatment. Although they repeatedly asked why Goold was on this course of treatment, they could not get any answer from his doctors or nurses. Finally, after six days, a nurse tried to reverse the course of care, but it was too late: Goold died the next day. "You wouldn't treat a dog the way my poor dad was treated," said Goold's daughter Susan Phillips. "We are all devastated, the best

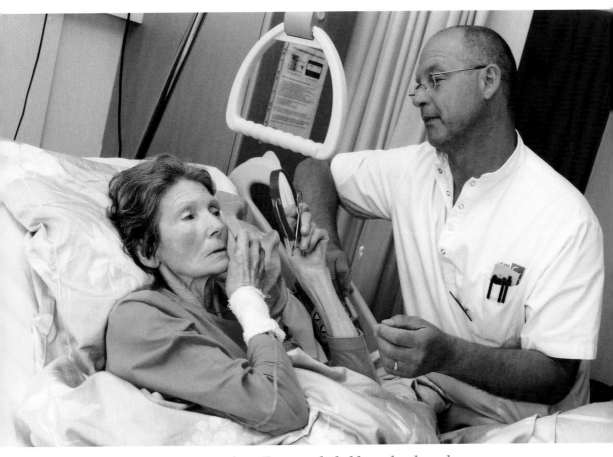

Until 2014, many hospitals in Britain abided by a death-and-dying protocol known as the Liverpool Care Pathway for the Dying Patient (LCP), a set of end-of-life guidelines that aimed to help hospitals give their dying patients the same high-quality palliative care that terminal patients get in a hospice facility.

interests of the patient was not starving him to death. My mum didn't even get to say goodbye to her husband of 51 years because she was too traumatised."[3]

Goold's case was one of several high-profile stories that eventually caused authorities to review the Liverpool Care Pathway and ultimately recommend it be discontinued. "There have been repeated instances of patients dying on the LCP being treated with less than the respect that they deserve," concluded a formal review commission put together by the Department of Health. "Where care is already poor, the LCP is sometimes used as a tick box [checklist] exercise, and good care of the dying patient and their relatives or carers may be absent."[4] The overall failure of the LCP was attributed to inadequate or inconsistent staff training and hospitals' need to distribute resources in an efficient manner (for example, there were complaints that some hospitals prioritized the treatment of patients who were more likely to recover and placed less importance on helping patients who were less likely to survive). In July 2013 the commission recommended that the LCP be phased out by early 2014.

For some, the abolition of the LCP was proof that end-of-life protocols should never replace medical treatment and care that aims to heal. "There is no objective criteria to say whether a person is dying or not—there is no scientific way to know, and that means the system is open to terrific abuse," says Patrick Pullicino, a British neurologist who opposed implementation of the LCP. "If you stop treating someone for their condition they are unlikely to improve. If, on top of that, you sedate them heavily, you are unlikely to see any improvement even if it does occur. That is why putting patients on the pathway becomes a self-fulfilling prophecy."[5] Yet for others, the demise of the LCP reflected not a failure of palliative care strategies but how much work needs to be done to improve them. As Dzeng puts it, "The Liverpool Care Pathway has met its end today, but the need to promote a peaceful and dignified death has never been more important."[6]

Whether end-of-life care should be guided by protocols or whether such protocols violate medical ethics and standards of care is one of the many debates explored in *Issues That Concern You: Death and Dying*. Approachable and clear pro/con article pairs also explore the role the government should have in end-of-life care; whether people have a right to die as they choose; whether physician-assisted suicide should be legal; and to what extent finances and economics should be considered when dealing with the end of life. Together they offer students an easily accessible collection of opinions on this serious issue.

Notes

1. Quoted in Bill Keller, "How to Die," *New York Times*, October 7, 2012. www.nytimes.com/2012/10/08/opinion/keller-how-to-die.html?pagewanted=all.
2. Elizabeth Dzeng, "Dying with Dignity—What Next After the Liverpool Care Pathway?," *Guardian* (Manchester, UK), July 16, 2013. www.guardian.co.uk/commentisfree/2013/jul/16/dying-liverpool-care-pathway.
3. Quoted in Rachel Allen, "Family's Anguish After Dad Was Starved to Death at Addenbrooke's Hospital on Liverpool Care Pathway," Cambridge News, June 3, 2013. www.cambridge-news.co.uk/News/Familys-anguish-after-dad-was-starved-to-death-at-Addenbrookes-Hospital-on-Liverpool-Care-Pathway-05032013.htm.
4. Gov.UK, *More Care, Less Pathway: A Review of the Liverpool Care Pathway*, July 2013, p. 3. www.gov.uk/government/uploads/system/uploads/attachment data/file/212450/Liverpool Care Pathway.pdf.
5. Quoted in Laura Donnelly, "Leading Doctor's Fears About Liverpool Care Pathway," *Sunday Telegraph* (London), March 3, 2013. www.telegraph.co.uk/health/healthnews/9904650/Leading-doctors-fears-about-Liverpool-Care-Pathway.html.
6. Dzeng, "Dying with Dignity."

ONE

End-of-Life Care Should Be Minimal and Swift

Ken Murray

In the following viewpoint Ken Murray argues that most lifesaving medical care offers little additional quality of life. He discusses how terminally ill doctors typically reject life-extending procedures because they know it will make little difference to their fate, prolong their suffering, and cost their families a lot of money. Murray says Americans should take a cue from their habits: If doctors are eschewing end-of-life care because of its futility and expense, so too should more American nonmedical persons. A good death, according to Murray, is one that is fast, inexpensive, and as painless and undramatic as possible. Americans can achieve such a death by creating specific end-of-life care plans and understanding that many procedures will not significantly increase their chances of quality survival.

Before he retired, Murray taught family medicine at the University of Southern California.

Years ago, Charlie, a highly respected orthopedist and a mentor of mine, found a lump in his stomach. It was diagnosed as pancreatic cancer by one of the best surgeons in the country, who had developed a procedure that could triple a patient's five-year-survival odds—from 5% to 15%—albeit with a poor quality of life.

Charlie, 68 years old, was uninterested. He went home the next day, closed his practice and never set foot in a hospital again. He focused on spending time with his family. Several months later, he died at home. He got no chemotherapy, radiation or surgical treatment. Medicare didn't spend much on him.

The Limits of Modern Medicine

It's not something that we like to talk about, but doctors die, too. What's unusual about them is not how much treatment they get compared with most Americans, but how little. They know exactly what is going to happen, they know the choices, and they generally have access to any sort of medical care that they could want. But they tend to go serenely and gently.

Doctors don't want to die any more than anyone else does. But they usually have talked about the limits of modern medicine with their families. They want to make sure that, when the time comes, no heroic measures are taken. During their last moments, they know, for instance, that they don't want someone breaking their ribs by performing cardiopulmonary resuscitation [CPR] (which is what happens when CPR is done right).

Death with Clarity

In a 2003 article, Joseph J. Gallo and others looked at what physicians want when it comes to end-of-life decisions. In a survey of 765 doctors, they found that 64% had created an advanced directive—specifying what steps should and should not be taken to save their lives should they become incapacitated. That compares to only about 20% for the general public. (As one might expect, older doctors are more likely than younger doctors to have made "arrangements," as shown in a study by Paula Lester and others.)

Why such a large gap between the decisions of doctors and patients? The case of CPR is instructive. A study by Susan

Diem and others of how CPR is portrayed on TV found that it was successful in 75% of the cases and that 67% of the TV patients went home. In reality, a 2010 study of more than 95,000 cases of CPR found that only 8% of patients survived for more than one month. Of these, only about 3% could lead a mostly normal life.

Unlike previous eras, when doctors simply did what they thought was best, our system is now based on what patients choose. Physicians really try to honor their patients' wishes, but when patients ask "What would you do?," we often avoid answering. We don't want to impose our views on the vulnerable.

"Lifesaving" Care Is Often Futile

The result is that more people receive futile "lifesaving" care, and fewer people die at home than did, say, 60 years ago. Nursing professor Karen Kehl, in an article called "Moving Toward Peace: An Analysis of the Concept of a Good Death," ranked the attributes of a graceful death, among them: being comfortable and in control, having a sense of closure, making the most of relationships and having family involved in care. Hospitals today provide few of these qualities.

Written directives can give patients far more control over how their lives end. But while most of us accept that taxes are inescapable, death is a much harder pill to swallow, which keeps the vast majority of Americans from making proper arrangements.

It doesn't have to be that way. Several years ago, at age 60, my older cousin Torch (born at home by the light of a flashlight, or torch) had a seizure. It turned out to be the result of lung cancer that had gone to his brain. We learned that with aggressive treatment, including three to five hospital visits a week for chemotherapy, he would live perhaps four months.

Torch was no doctor, but he knew that he wanted a life of quality, not just quantity. Ultimately, he decided against any treatment and simply took pills for brain swelling. He moved in with me.

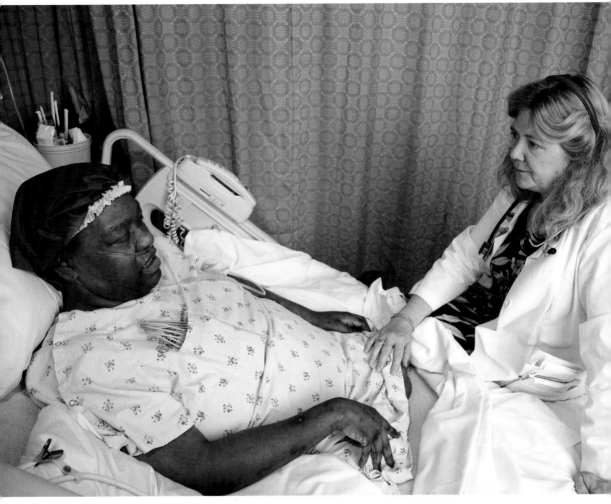

The author argues that people can achieve a "good death" by creating specific end-of-life care plans and recognizing that many medical procedures will not significantly increase their chances of survival or quality of life.

A Good Death Is Swift

We spent the next eight months having fun together like we hadn't had in decades. We went to Disneyland, his first time, and we hung out at home. Torch was a sports nut, and he was very happy to watch sports and eat my cooking. He had no serious pain, and he remained high-spirited.

How Doctors Want to Die

The Johns Hopkins Precursors Study is an ongoing health survey. As part of the decades-long effort to assess health and care, it asked physicians about what technologies or interventions they would want if they fell seriously ill. Their answers—which differ from the general public's—are indicative of the usefulness and appropriateness of end-of-life care.

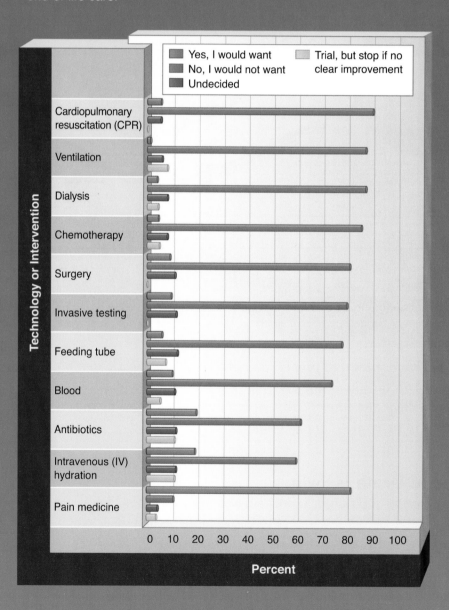

Taken from: Johns Hopkins Precursors Study; "The Bitter End." RadioLab.com, January 15, 2013.

One day, he didn't wake up. He spent the next three days in a coma-like sleep and then died. The cost of his medical care for those eight months, for the one drug he was taking, was about $20.

As for me, my doctor has my choices on record. They were easy to make, as they are for most physicians. There will be no heroics, and I will go gentle into that good night. Like my mentor Charlie. Like my cousin Torch. Like so many of my fellow doctors.

TWO

End-of-Life Care Should Not Necessarily Be Minimal and Swift

Cynthia Jones-Nosacek

Cynthia Jones-Nosacek is a family-practice physician who frequently speaks and writes on medical ethics and related issues. In the following viewpoint she argues that end-of-life care is a personal, heartrending process that takes time to get right. She acknowledges that end-of-life care is outrageously expensive and often cannot cure the terminal disease. But it also offers people hope that their situation will improve, which in her opinion is very valuable. Jones-Nosacek also thinks prolonged end-of-life care is worth it because it offers a person a few additional years or months of time to make memories with their loved ones. It takes time for a person to articulate what exactly their medical priorities are, she says, and it is hard for both the dying and their family members to say good-bye. For all of these reasons, she thinks end-of-life care should not be rushed or minimal; rather, it should be as extensive and involved as the dying person wishes.

I am a family physician. I see patients in the office, at the hospital, in the nursing home and even hospice. Some of them have been seeing me for over 25 years. I am also the daughter of a woman who spent all but a week of the last 2 1/2 months of her life in the hospital, much of that time in the ICU [intensive care unit]. My interest in end-of-life care is both professional and personal.

The Sunday *Crossroads* op-ed "We must learn to let go" by Minneapolis internist Craig Bowron makes it look easy. If you are old and sick, you should resign yourself to dying. And if your family does not let you die, you will linger in pain. All that money wasted. Studies show that elderly who are at the end of their lives are six times more expensive to care for than those who are not; 5% of Medicare recipients take up 25% of the total yearly Medicare costs. As we get older, bodily systems fail, becoming more expensive and complicated to maintain. That is only logical. But Bowron's underlying assumption is that it is a life not worth living.

The author believes prolonged or extraordinary end-of-life care offers people a few additional years or months of time in which to make memories with their loved ones.

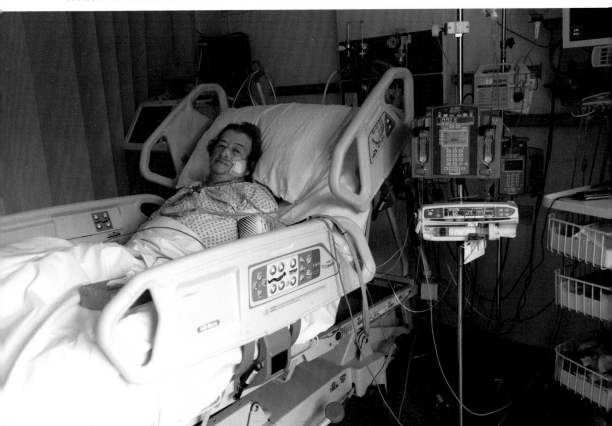

Americans Could Be Better Informed About End-of-Life Options

The Economist Intelligence Unit's Quality of Death index measures public awareness of end-of-life care, which varies across the globe. Belgium, Ireland, and the United Kingdom (UK) rank highest when it comes to evidence of public discussions about end-of-life care. China ranks last. The United States ranks relatively poorly in this respect, reflecting a lack of awareness among Americans of hospice services and end-of-life care in general (much of which takes place in the home).

Public Awareness of End-of-Life Care

Highest ranking (excellent)			Lowest ranking (poor)	
5	4	3	2	1
Belgium	Australia	Canada	Brazil	China
Ireland	Austria	Czech Republic	Finland	
UK	France	Denmark	Greece	
	Hungary	Germany	India	
	Japan	Hong Kong	Italy	
	South Korea	Iceland	Luxembourg	
	Netherlands	Malaysia	Mexico	
	New Zealand	Poland	Portugal	
	Norway	Singapore	Russia	
	Sweden	Slovakia	Switzerland	
	Taiwan	South Africa	Turkey	
	Uganda	Spain		
		United States		

Taken from: Economist Intelligence Unit. "The Quality of Death: Ranking End-of-Life Care Across the World," 2010.

Figuring Out What Is Right Takes Time

Real life is messier. Consider: An elderly man, whose only medical problem was high blood pressure, was diagnosed with an incurable brain tumor. Treatment would give him at most six to 12 months to live. By electing treatment, his last few months of life were the bulk of his lifetime Medicare expenses. But the treatment would hopefully give him the ability to speak again—to tell his wife and family how much he loved them, to give them all those extra days.

In my mother's case, it was serious infection that sent her to the hospital. She went in with a living will that said no ventilator, but when faced with the possibility that she might need one temporarily while her lungs healed, she changed her mind. She was in and out of the ICU three times those last few months. But there was always hope, a chance that she would go home again.

When we found out that, unfortunately, the reason she was so ill was she had terminal cancer, we chose hospice and took her home. But it took over two months to figure it out.

It is not always easy to know what to do. And there is pain all around. Doctors, nurses, patients, family all suffer. If you are a hospitalist who only sees patients at their worst [while hospitalized], you never get to see the before or the after.

Extra Time Can Yield Important Memories

The last day my mother was in the hospital, I took a "before" picture to show the nurses what a vital woman she was. There are families who need time to see the truth, to let it sink in, especially if they are coming from a distance. There are those who refuse to give up hope—families who insist that their loved one could be saved, even when all the doctors say no. My mother begged for chemotherapy, even when she was told that it would not help. Her last words to me were, "I don't want to die."

We need to do more with palliative care for people with life-limiting illness: help to control their pain, minimize symptoms and help them to deal with the implications of their diagnosis. We need to, as I tell my patients, help them to live as full a life as possible with the time they have been given. Some studies show improved quality of life with decreased cost. But death and illness are still not always predictable.

And there is the family's pain to consider, long after the doctor has forgotten the case and moved on to others. They have to live with the decisions that were or were not made. A hundred years ago, there was less we could do. And while people died at home, it was not necessarily peaceful.

People with cancer died in agony, with pneumonia and heart failure gasping for breath, from starvation because they could not swallow after their stroke. My great-grandfather died a lingering death from gangrene caused by a fall from a barn roof. Maybe we can only give the elderly a few extra years, but the memories we give the surviving family members are not always bad, the life not always one of continual suffering.

Let People Decide

Bowron gave us the example of the man who had [had] a stroke and multiple medical problems, but we do not know how it ended. Did he survive? With aggressive treatment, did the stroke end up being less devastating than initially thought? Or did the man end up forgotten, alone in a nursing home, abandoned by his family who wanted to remember him as he was? Or, after working through the grief of his loss of mobility, did he again begin to enjoy the sunrise and the gurgle of his grandbabies? And, most important, what was that man's decision? People with mild dementia can make their decisions about how they want to live. What did he want?

In [Charles Dickens's] "A Christmas Carol," the Ghost of Christmas Present tells Ebenezer Scrooge that we should "forbear . . . until you have discovered What the surplus is, and Where it is. Will you decide what men shall live, what men shall die? It may be, that . . . you are less fit to live than millions like (Tiny Tim)." Especially for life and death, we need to know who that "surplus" is. It could be your mother.

THREE

Taking Responsibility for Death

Susan Jacoby

> In the following viewpoint Susan Jacoby explains why she
> thinks financial matters should influence end-of-life care
> decisions. She says that most end-of-life care offers a person
> little in terms of quality of life or extended survival yet costs
> tens of thousands of dollars. Most dying people do not want
> to burden their loved ones with huge bills upon their death;
> most prefer to die efficiently and leave their families good
> memories rather than debt. Jacoby says no one should feel
> pressured to go without medical care because of its cost; yet,
> at the same time, they should feel a duty to refuse expensive
> medical care that is unnecessary and will not improve their
> quality or length of life. Together, she says, Americans can
> reduce society's overwhelming medical expenses by weigh-
> ing their costs against their benefits.
>
> Jacoby is an author of nonfiction books, including
> *Never Say Die: The Myth and Marketing of the New Old
> Age* and *The Age of American Unreason*.

I was standing by my 89-year-old mother's hospital bed when she
asked a doctor, "Is there anything you can do here to give me
back the life I had last year, when I wasn't in pain every minute?"

The young medical resident, stunned by the directness of the question, blurted out, "Honestly, ma'am, no."

And so Irma Broderick Jacoby went home and lived another year, during which she never again entered a hospital or subjected herself to an invasive, expensive medical procedure. The pain of multiple degenerative diseases was eased by prescription drugs, and she died last November [2011] after two weeks in a hospice, on terms determined by explicit legal instructions and discussions with her children—no respirators, no artificial feeding, no attempts to buy one more day for a body that would not let her turn over in bed or swallow without agony.

The hospice room and pain-relieving palliative care cost only about $400 a day, while the average hospital stay costs Medicare over $6,000 a day. Although Mom's main concern was her comfort and dignity, she also took satisfaction in not running up Medicare payments for unwanted treatments and not leaving private medical bills for her children to pay. A third of the Medicare budget is now spent in the last year of life, and a third of that goes for care in the last month. Those figures would surely be lower if more Americans, while they were still healthy, took the initiative to spell out what treatments they do—and do not—want by writing living wills and appointing health care proxies.

As the aging baby boom generation places unprecedented demands on the health care system, there is little ordinary citizens can do—witness the tortuous arguments in the Supreme Court this week over the constitutionality of the Affordable Care Act—to influence either the cost or the quality of the treatment they receive. However, end-of-life planning is one of the few actions within the power of individuals who wish to help themselves and their society. Too few Americans are shouldering this responsibility.

Of course many people want more aggressive treatment than my mother. And advance directives aren't "death panels"; they can also be used to ensure the deployment of every tool of modern medicine. They can be changed or withdrawn at any time by a mentally competent person.

Americans worry more about the financial burden of falling seriously ill than they do about not being emotionally or spiritually prepared for death.

Question: "On a scale of 0–10, how much do the following issues concern you (where 0 means it does not concern you at all and 10 means it concerns you a great deal)?"

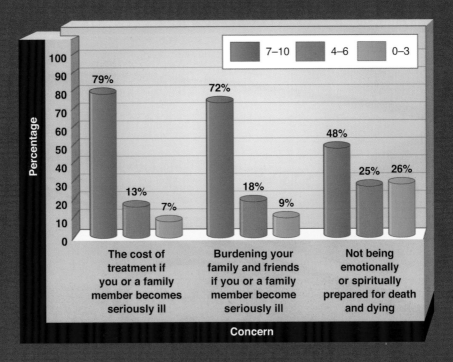

Taken from: *The National Journal* and the Regence Foundation. "Living Well at the End of Life: A National Conversation," February 2011.

But public opinion polls consistently show that most Americans, like my mother, worry about too much rather than too little medical intervention. In a Pew Research Center poll released in 2006, only 22 percent said a doctor should always try to save a patient's life, while 70 percent believed that patients should sometimes be allowed to die. More than half said they would tell their doctor to end treatment if they were in great pain with no hope of improvement.

Yet only 69 percent had discussed end-of-life care with a spouse; just 17 percent, or 40 percent of those over 65, had done

Jacoby argues that no one should feel pressured to go without medical care because of its cost, yet, at the same time, everyone should feel it a duty to refuse expensive medical care that is unnecessary and will not improve quality of living or length of life.

so with their children. One-third of Americans had a living will and even fewer have taken the more legally enforceable measure of appointing a health care proxy to act on their behalf if they cannot act for themselves.

The latter omission is especially disturbing because by 2030, more than 8.5 million Americans will be over 85—an age at which roughly half will suffer from Alzheimer's disease or some other form of irreversible dementia. For many members of the baby boom generation—more likely to be divorced and childless than their parents—there may be no legal next of kin.

Without advance directives, even a loving child may be ignorant of her parent's wishes. My mother remained conscious and in charge of her care until just a few days before she died, but like most women over 85, she was a widow. My younger brother died of pancreatic cancer two weeks before she did. It was an immense comfort to me, at a terrible time, to have no doubts about what she wanted.

My mother drew up her directives in the 1980s, when she was a volunteer in the critical care lounge of her local hospital. She once watched, appalled, as an adult daughter threw a coffeepot at her brother for suggesting that their comatose mother's respirator be turned off. Because the siblings could not agree and the patient had no living will, she was kept hooked up to machines for another two weeks at a cost (then) of nearly $80,000 to Medicare and $20,000 to her family—even though her doctors agreed there was no hope.

The worst imaginable horror for my mother was that she might be kept alive by expensive and painful procedures when she no longer had a functioning brain. She was equally horrified by the idea of family fights around her deathbed. "I don't want one of you throwing a coffeepot at the other," she told us in a half-joking, half-serious fashion.

There is a clear contradiction between the value that American society places on personal choice and Americans' reluctance to make their own decisions, insofar as possible, about the care they will receive as death nears. Obviously, no one likes to think about sickness and death. But the politicization of end-of-life planning and its entwinement with religion-based culture wars provide extra, irrational obstacles to thinking ahead when it matters most.

As someone over 65, I do not consider it my duty to die for the convenience of society. I do consider it my duty, to myself and younger generations, to follow the example my mother set by doing everything in my power to ensure that I will never be the object of medical intervention that cannot restore my life but can only prolong a costly living death.

FOUR

Economics Should Not Influence End-of-Life Care Decisions

Mike Stopa

In the following viewpoint Mike Stopa argues that government health care legislation inappropriately emphasizes the cost of end-of-life medical care over people's health and wishes. He discusses government efforts to get people to plan ahead for their deaths, warning that such initiatives reflect the government's interest in curbing the costs of such care, not necessarily providing people with high-quality care or the kind of care that is right for them and their families. Stopa worries that people are increasingly being pressured to choose less-expensive health care options that compromise their health and freedom. He also worries that government efforts to curb costs limit innovation and medical advances, which thrive in the free market. For all of these reasons, he argues that economics should not affect end-of-life decisions and that the government should stay out of people's health care decisions.

Stopa is a nanophysics researcher at Harvard University.

Supporters of President [Barack] Obama's health care reform law have relentlessly derided [former Alaska governor] Sarah Palin's notion of "death panels" [presumably made up of bureaucrats deciding who is worthy of coverage] as a vulgar rhetorical technique, with no basis in reality, devised merely to scare a gullible, uneducated citizenry into rallying to repeal the law. The death panel notion persists, however, because it denotes, in a pithy way, the economic realities of scarcity inherent in nationalizing a rapidly developing, high-technology industry on which people's lives depend in a rather immediate way. [Nineteenth-century author] G.K. Chesterton once wrote that vulgar notions (and jokes) invariably contain a "subtle and spiritual idea." The subtle and spiritual idea behind "death panels" is that life-prolonging medical technology is an expensive, limited commodity and if the market doesn't determine who gets it, someone else will.

Pressuring People to Put Cost Ahead of Care

In December [2010], the Center for Medicare and Medicaid Services issued a regulation, since rescinded by the Obama administration, that would have allowed doctors to be reimbursed for "voluntary advanced care" planning. When the regulation was publicized, it resulted in a renewed outcry that such end-of-life planning provisions presage the inevitable death panels of ObamaCare [a derisive nickname for the Patient Protection and Affordable Care Act].

In response, J. Donald Schumacher, president and CEO of the National Hospice and Palliative Care Organization, wrote in a CNN [Cable News Network] opinion piece that "an advance care planning consultation is not about limiting or rationing care. It's not about hastening death. It's not about having choices made for the patient. It's not about saving money."

But anyone who thinks that end-of-life planning has nothing to do with cost has never had the unenviable experience of participating in that planning. According to Donald Berwick, the head of the Center for Medicare and Medicaid Services, "Using unwanted procedures in terminal illness is a form of assault. In economic terms, it is waste. Several techniques, including advance directives and involvement of patients and families in decision-making, have been shown to reduce inappropriate care at the end of life, leading to both lower cost and more humane care."

J. Donald Schumacher (far right), president and CEO of the National Hospice and Palliative Care Organization, takes part in testimony before the US Senate. Schumacher asserts that an advance-care planning consultation is not about limiting or rationing care, hastening death, making someone else's choices, or saving money.

The resistance to incorporating end-of-life planning into Medicare is based on the rational fear that such planning will be used to coax patients into forgoing life-extending technologies that Medicare administrators may deem risky, of marginal benefit, or unlikely to succeed—an estimation that could be based in part on the cost of the technology.

Americans Think Finances Should Not Drive End-of-Life Care

According to a national poll taken jointly by the *National Journal* and the Regence Foundation, the majority of Americans think the health care system should spend whatever it takes to extend people's lives.

Question: "With which of the following statements do you agree more?"

37%
"The health care system spends far too much time trying to extend the lives of seriously ill patients, which diverts resources from other priorities, adds to our country's financial difficulties, and increases the cost of health care for everyone."

55%
"The health care system in this country has the responsibility, the medical technology, and the expertise to offer treatments to seriously ill patients and spend whatever it takes to extend their lives."

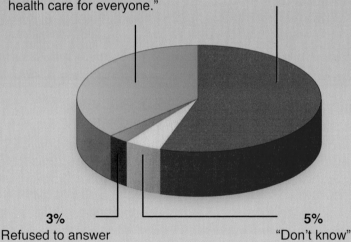

3%
Refused to answer

5%
"Don't know"

Taken from: *National Journal* and the Regence Foundation. "Living Well at the End of Life: A National Conversation," February 2011. http://syndication.nationaljournal.com/communications/NationalJournalRegence Toplines.pdf.

The Goal Is to Save Money

Moreover, the suspicion that such programmed advance planning conceals ulterior motives is exacerbated by the fact that relatively few patients will ultimately benefit from it. It is mainly of value for those who do not die suddenly, who have no trustworthy relations to maintain their power of decision, and who lose their wits a potentially long time before their death.

Opposition to government-funded end-of-life planning does not imply ignorance of the indignity or discomfort of having one more tube placed into one's body to buy an extra few days of painful life. (Although one can imagine concluding that dignity is a highly overrated virtue when the alternative is death). But when a massive government bureaucracy, tasked with determining medical "best practices" and controlling costs, announces a policy that "wellness visits" should have us chatting with our doctors about what technologically invasive, life-extending procedures we would just as happily do without, we are not supposed to be suspicious?

Even aside from end-of-life counseling, any form of medical insurance, including ObamaCare, has to determine where the boundaries of coverage lie. Today, hospitals decide not to provide life-extending procedures all the time. In practice, for those who have no independent means, some form of utilitarian, "greatest good for greatest number" ethic is imposed whereby treatment is approved based on things like the likelihood of success and the potential lifespan of the patient. Much of the rigor of those considerations is already envisioned as part of the Patient-Centered Outcomes Research Institute.

Patients Lose When Care Is a Commodity

Conversely, medical technology is forever inventing new medicines and procedures that have the potential to extend life or cure the previously incurable. Each such technique inevitably passes through a phase where it is experimental, risky, and expensive. Often enough the sky is the limit and so late in life we are all liable to become, in the words of the late Harvard philosopher Robert Nozick, "utility monsters."

To the extent that ObamaCare ultimately succeeds in imposing uniformity on basic health care, it will likely lead to the creation of secondary markets for providing insurance against various health eventualities and access to "heroic" procedures to extend life. Water runs downhill and it's a good thing that it does. First, we need to have people buy the expensive medicines and experimental technologies. Europe has discovered this as its regulated system of medicine has driven its pharmaceutical industry farther and farther behind that of the United States. Capping costs kills innovation.

But, in addition, Palin is right. Death panels are an inevitable consequence of socialized medicine. The law of scarcity demands them.

A mature discussion of health care must recognize basic economics so that we can think ahead on how to satisfy the demands of those who are not satisfied with base-level care.

FIVE

The Government Should Ration End-of-Life Care

M. Gregg Bloche

M. Gregg Bloche is a physician and a law professor at Georgetown University in Washington, D.C. In the following viewpoint he points out that Americans are ambivalent when it comes to health care—on the one hand, they demand that doctors go to all lengths to keep them and their loved ones alive and healthy; yet on the other, they demand that health care costs be low and affordable. They cannot have it both ways, contends Bloche: Giving everyone any kind of care they demand creates costs the country cannot sustain. Therefore, he argues, health care must be rationed, or doled out on an as-needed basis. It makes fiscal and moral sense to spend health care dollars on the people who will benefit the most he says, and to withhold expensive care when it is unlikely to improve a person's chances of survival or quality of life. He concludes that this is the only way to avoid ballooning medical costs that will eventually bankrupt the country.

Several years ago, I was asked to speak on end-of-life issues at a retreat for Southern California physicians. A number of doctors there brought up one particular case: an 82-year-old woman who'd suffered a massive heart attack while visiting her daughter.

Her story captures the difficult choices that keep us from controlling healthcare spending. Unless we all confront those choices, the costs of medical care will consume us, stealing away an ever-larger share of our national wealth and driving federal budget deficits to catastrophic levels.

When the Battle Cannot Be Won

The patient was admitted to intensive care, then put on "pressors"—medications that boost blood pressure by causing muscle cells surrounding tiny arteries to contract. Her doctors quickly concluded that her prognosis was dismal. Aggressive doses failed to raise her systolic pressure [the top number in a blood pressure reading] above 70 (a worrisome sign). Too much heart muscle was nonfunctioning. Yet she remained awake, alert and chatty.

The woman's daughter was around when the doctors delivered their dire prognosis. The pressors were pointless, they said; the battle couldn't be won. Their prescription was to end aggressive treatment. The patient didn't obviously object to the doctors' plan, but her daughter, a social worker told me, "felt it was an assault."

The daughter began paying close attention to clinical details. She questioned the doctors about their intentions. The doctors, in turn, grew annoyed.

"Her daughter could not let go," one of them later told me, "even in the face of a bad prognosis. She was taking . . . an adversarial position, almost litigious. What I tried to clarify for her was that this was not an adversarial relationship."

But one of the doctors admitted to some thinking that wouldn't have reassured the daughter: "When we see dollars wasted, that's not a good thing. Nobody presents that to the patient." Keeping the mother alive, which required the high-tech monitoring and ministrations of the ICU [intensive care unit], was most likely a waste because her chances for survival were so tiny. "The problem is that individual members only care about themselves, because they don't have the global perspective."

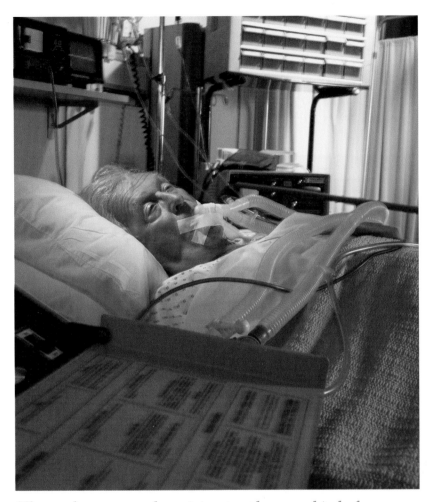

The author argues that giving people every kind of care they demand creates costs the country cannot sustain. Therefore, health care must be rationed, or doled out on an as-needed basis.

One cardiologist did present this perspective to the patient. According to colleagues, he came to her bedside, told her she didn't have enough heart muscle to survive, then said: "Have you ever stayed in a really expensive hotel, like the Plaza? You know how expensive a room is? Six to eight hundred dollars. Well, you know how expensive this room is? Ten thousand dollars."

The Expensive Few

Just 10 percent of the 24 million Medicare beneficiaries who received any inpatient or outpatient hospital care in 2009 accounted for 64 percent of the cost. Some say the enormous cost of end-of-life care is impossible to sustain.

Medicare's Average Spending on Hospital Care, by Age

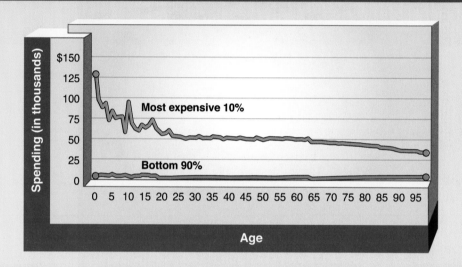

Medicare's Total Spending on Hospital Care, by Age

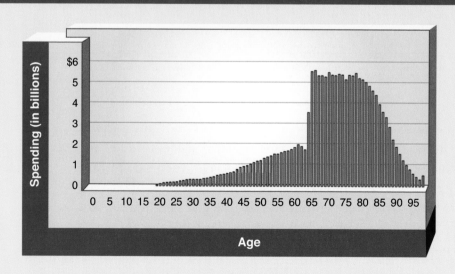

Taken from: Janet Adamy and Tom McGinty. "The Crashing Cost of Care." *Wall Street Journal*, July 6, 2012.

Giving Everyone Everything Will Bankrupt Us

The daughter threatened to sue, demanded new doctors and insisted that the staff go all-out to keep her mom alive. Four weeks later, the 82-year-old patient left the hospital on foot. For a year or so, until she died, she divided her time between her daughter's home, an assisted living facility and her own residence.

The doctor who'd complained to me about the daughter's "adversarial position" said her mother's survival astonished him. Yet he stands by the decision he'd have preferred: to take her off pressors and get her out of the ICU—in effect, to let her die. "If you say that the fact that this lady survived means we should do that type of thing for every patient—I'm not prepared to say that," he said.

And then he spoke the unspeakable: "We are subconsciously rationing care, whether we call it that or believe that's what we're doing. . . . If we didn't, the reality is that we would be facing an absurdity in which we made . . . near-futile efforts to save one life out of an enormous number of failures. We'd bankrupt our healthcare system."

Americans Unrealistically Want It All

We want our doctors to go all-out for our loved ones and ourselves. But as voters and consumers, we send a different message. We pick politicians who promise to cut taxes, and we demand low-cost insurance. We're telling government and the healthcare industry to hold the line on healthcare costs, even if it means sacrificing clinical benefits. And we put doctors in the middle of this contradiction.

In recent weeks [spring 2011], private insurers have revealed plans for double-digit rate hikes. Our medical bills are already close to a fifth of our national income, on track to reach one-third within 25 years. Soaring Medicare and Medicaid costs are the main reason for nightmarish federal deficit projections over the long term. Yet as Republicans and Democrats battle over the federal budget to the point of threatening a government shutdown, serious healthcare spending cuts remain unspeakable.

House Budget Committee Chairman Rep. Paul Ryan (R-Wis.) [in 2011] proposed to cut Medicare and Medicaid by shifting their costs to poor and middle-class Americans who can't afford them. It's an unconscionable approach, but it at least acknowledges the urgency of gaining control over federal healthcare spending. Neither President [Barack] Obama nor congressional Democrats have put forth plausible proposals for doing so.

How might we "bend the curve" of rising costs without forcing doctors to break with Hippocratic ideals [namely, to do everything they can to help and not harm the patient]? Percentage points can be trimmed by better coordinating care and providing it more efficiently. But the main driver behind rising costs is indiscriminate adoption of new technology.

Clear Limits Must Be Set

We must make it much harder for high-cost clinical wizardry to become part of our expectations. We should distinguish between decisive advances—biological breakthroughs that make large therapeutic leaps possible—and technologies that dazzle but deliver only marginal results. We can do this by demanding proof that pricey services add value before permitting health-care providers to tap insurers for payment. And we can harness intellectual property law to encourage therapeutic leaps by giving longer-lasting patents to more effective tests and treatments. We should also stop paying providers more for using technology than for listening and talking to their patients.

But as a society, we also have to set limits when it comes to individual treatment. We can't afford to spend without restraint in the ICU, in pursuit of tiny chances. We must—and this is the hardest part—decide what we can and can't afford. We have to let politicians and policymakers grapple truthfully with these issues rather than punishing them for "killing Grandma" when they speak of making hard choices about healthcare.

We accept cost-benefit tradeoffs in other realms: We base airline and occupational safety regulations on dollar figures for the

© Glenn and Gary McCoy/Distributed by Universal Uclick via CartoonStock.com.

value of life. Similar clarity must replace the vague terms (like "medical necessity") that insurers use to veil healthcare rationing. Clear limits, applicable to all, can help us come to terms with the need to say "no" without shattering our trust in medicine.

Bedside rationing on the sly won't do.

SIX

Terminally Ill People Do Not Have the Right to Die When and How They Want

Fritz Spencer

Fritz Spencer is the former editor of the *Record*, a publication of the Christian Civic League. In the following viewpoint he argues that no one has the right to take his or her own life, even the dying. He argues that there is no right to self-destruction; humanity's greatest thinkers have concluded that if life is to have any value, it must be protected at all costs. In Spencer's opinion, life is a gift from God—therefore, only God can decide who lives and who dies. He warns that legalizing physician-assisted suicide—that is, allowing doctors to prescribe a fatal dose of medication that terminally ill patients can take if they want to end their suffering—not only devalues life but has the potential to be used to pressure all kinds of vulnerable people to end their lives, even against their wishes. Spencer concludes that life is precious and sacred, and any form of unnatural death should never be condoned or sanctioned.

A splendid fire sparkles in the eyes of our loved ones, a fire brighter, clearer and more charming than the light of any star. But when that fire burns low and dies out forever, little is left except the memory of a kind voice or a haunting glance from a torn and tattered photo.

Modern medicine boasts of its many conquests over disease, but no doctor has yet subdued the most ancient and formidable enemy of mankind. Nor has any scientist wrested a single inch of territory from this grim and relentless foe. Between the sick

Jack Kevorkian's "Thanatron" was called by his detractors the "Death Machine." Kevorkian was sentenced to ten to twenty-five years in prison for using it to help terminally ill patients commit suicide.

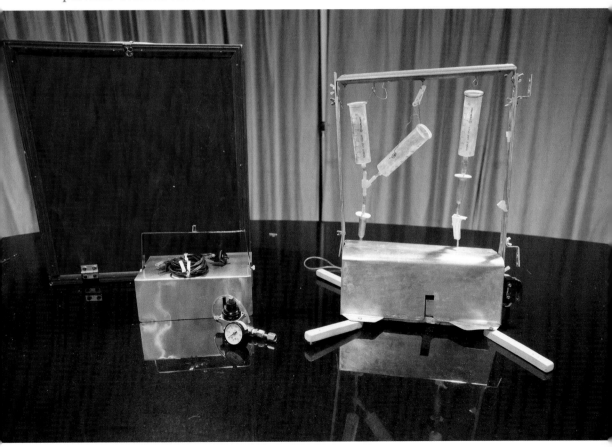

patient and the enemy stands a battery of tests, row upon row of test tubes, million-dollar devices to scan the battleground and pinpoint the enemy, chemicals to wither and wear him down and scalpels to hold him at bay. But come he will. And he will arrive in the form of an irreversible calamity.

No Right to Self-Destruction Can Ever Exist

"Physician-assisted suicide" is a pleasant-sounding euphemism for what earlier generations called "mercy killing." The term "mercy killing" is preferable, because it brings the ugly reality out of the shadows and into the light of day. Suicide, even when done to end suffering, is self-murder; and no one has the right to take an innocent life. Hence "mercy killing" is currently a crime under the Maine Criminal Code, as it is in all states. Oregon, Washington and Montana have made an exception in the case of physician-assisted suicide.

These laws prohibiting suicide, or aiding others to commit suicide, reflect the thinking of our greatest ethicists, theologians and secular thinkers. They have concluded that no right to self-destruction can ever exist.

The theologian argues that each human life is a gift from God. God grants the right to life, and the corresponding responsibility to preserve one's life rests with the individual. The philosopher reasons that life is not something over which man can have control.

A Slippery Slope Toward Devaluing Life

We do not have to rely on abstract ideas to know that physician-assisted suicide is wrong. If society legalizes mercy killing, the cry will go up to aid those suffering from Alzheimer's, Lou Gehrig's Disease and other diseases that render a patient incapable of making an informed decision. From there, it is only a short step to euthanizing those who are "unworthy of life." That is the irrefutable lesson of history; and it is a dire warning not to legalize euthanasia for any reason.

A case in point is Dr. Jack Kevorkian, a doctor who assisted in more than 100 suicides. He used two devices, one of which he

Physician-Assisted Suicide Is the Most Divisive Moral Issue Among Americans

According to a 2011 Gallup poll, physician-assisted suicide is the most divisive issue in the United States, with Americans closely split over whether it is morally acceptable or morally wrong. Stronger public consensus exists on sixteen other issues tested.

US Perceived Moral Acceptability of Behaviors and Social Policies

Behaviors and Social Policies	Morally acceptable	Morally wrong	Difference (percentage points)
Doctor-assisted suicide	45%	48%	3
Abortion	39%	51%	12
Having a baby outside of marriage	54%	41%	13
Buying and wearing clothing made of animal fur	56%	39%	17
Gay or lesbian relations	56%	39%	17
Medical testing on animals	55%	38%	17
Sex between an unmarried man and woman	60%	36%	24
Cloning animals	32%	62%	30
Medical research using stem cells obtained from human embryos	62%	30%	32
Gambling	64%	31%	33
Pornography	30%	66%	36
The death penalty	65%	28%	37
Divorce	69%	23%	46
Suicide	15%	80%	65
Cloning humans	12%	84%	72
Polygamy, when a married person has more than one spouse at the same time	11%	86%	75
Married men and women having an affair	7%	91%	84

*Ranked by "Difference"

Taken from: Gallup, May 5–8, 2011.

called his "Mercy Machine," an invention too gruesome to be described here. Suffice it to say that with each assisted suicide Kevorkian grew bolder, until he eventually injected a terminally ill patient with lethal drugs. For that crime, Kevorkian was sentenced to 10–25 years in prison.

Kevorkian obtained an early release from prison on compassionate grounds. Suffering from Hepatitis C and liver cancer, Kevorkian did not choose physician-assisted suicide. He chose to live on and die a natural death.

Only God Should Determine Who Lives and Dies

If physician-assisted suicide is legalized, society must not only weed out the Kevorkians. Society must also make sure that the panels reviewing each case never make an error about the course and outcome of a disease. The members of these panels must also be free from any economic, political and personal motive. Moreover, the doctors and lawyers who make up these panels must be able to see into the soul of each patient asking for an end to life.

In short, society must require that such panels are omniscient, infallible and morally perfect. In order for such panels to be successful, they must be free from the defects which are part of human nature. This is only reasonable, since we are asking them to do a job which properly belongs only to God.

SEVEN

Legalizing Physician-Assisted Suicide Will Lead to Abuse and Coerced Death

Seán P. O'Malley

Cardinal Seán P. O'Malley is the Roman Catholic archbishop of Boston, Massachusetts. In the following viewpoint he warns that physician-assisted suicide wrongly values death over life. Allowing people to legally kill themselves with a doctor's help threatens the most vulnerable members of society, such as the elderly, the disabled, and the very ill. O'Malley says these groups will feel pressured to kill themselves to relieve their families of the burden of caring for them or to save on their medical bills. In addition, he says, any kind of suicide is antithetical to the doctor-patient relationship; a doctor's priority must always be to heal or soothe the patient and never to intentionally kill them. Finally, legalized assisted suicide encourages dying rather than living, which in O'Malley's opinion is immoral. For all of these reasons he argues against legalizing physician-assisted suicide.

Proponents of physician-assisted suicide [PAS] tell us that there is no danger of a slippery slope, that in Oregon [where PAS is legal] the cases are "not that numerous" and are "carefully monitored." I hope that reasonable people will question these claims and reflect further on whether a law with insufficient safeguards is what we want in the commonwealth [of Massachusetts].

The Slippery Slope of Assisted Suicide

Slippery slope arguments involve small decisions that lead to undesirable outcomes that never would have been supported at the outset. Often, it is impossible to prove that one small step will have significant negative effects, but common sense allows reasonable people to judge the likelihood that a sequence of events that have happened in one place are likely to happen in another place in a similar way.

Question 2 [on the 2012 state ballot, which was voted down] proposes to allow physician-assisted suicide for those diagnosed with a terminal illness with six months or less to live. Many groups are concerned that, if passed, it not only would be harmful in itself, but could lead to unintended tragic outcomes. (1) Elder advocates are concerned that it could become a new form of elder abuse. (2) Advocates for the disabled are concerned it could lead to "quality of life" standards in our society, where those with a lower perceived quality of life receive fewer benefits or protections. (3) Doctors and nurses are concerned it could lead to a lower "quality of care" for those at the end of life. (4) Doctors are also concerned that it could undermine the doctor-patient relationship. (5) Ethicists are concerned that it could lead to a devaluing of human life. (6) Suicide-prevention organizations are concerned that the state legally allowing suicide for one group (those with terminal diagnoses of fewer than six months to live) could lead to increased suicide rates for the rest of the population. (7) Those who have studied the evolution of this matter in the Netherlands are concerned that assisted suicide could lead, first to voluntary euthanasia (requesting direct help to end one's life), and then to involuntary euthanasia (where a third-party determines that, if the patient were in his right mind, he would choose euthanasia).

Asserting that something could happen is not the same as stating that something will happen. Here are some facts that lead the groups above to be concerned. Please judge for yourself whether you agree with the risk that one or all of these concerns might occur in Massachusetts if we took the first step this Election Day by voting to legalize assisted suicide.

The Vulnerable Will Be Pressured to Kill Themselves

It could lead to increased elder abuse: Data on the crime of elder abuse show that perpetrators are frequently a spouse or an adult relative. Question 2 does not have safeguards to prevent an unscrupulous heir or indifferent family member from pressuring a sick person, either directly or in subtle ways, to end his or her life. That hardly gives sick people "greater freedom" and "enhanced autonomy" at the end of their lives.

It could lead to adoption of "quality of life" standards: Advocacy groups for the disabled are concerned that a policy of assisted suicide will inevitably lead to establishing social standards of acceptable life. When "quality of life" becomes more important than life itself, the mentally ill, the disabled, the depressed, and those who cannot defend themselves will be at risk of being targeted for assisted suicide, and perhaps eventually, for euthanasia. They fear that misunderstandings and false compassion could result in their being considered "better off dead," devalued, and treated as second class citizens in respect to their medical care.

Undermining the Doctor-Patient Relationship

It could lead to lower quality of care: Doctors' and nurses' groups have expressed concern that efforts to enhance hospice and palliative care will be weakened if a "lazy" path to end-of-life care like physician-assisted suicide is chosen by voters. They share grave concerns that medical cost-containment pressures will lead to a preference for a $100 prescription for lethal drugs over more expensive treatments.

It could undermine the doctor-patient relationship: The American Medical Association (AMA) and Massachusetts

Boston's Roman Catholic archbishop, Cardinal Seán P. O'Malley (pictured), believes that allowing people to legally kill themselves with a doctor's help endangers the most vulnerable members of society.

Medical Society oppose physician-assisted suicide because it violates the Hippocratic Oath to "do no harm" and changes the nature of the doctor's role of healing and comforting the patient. The AMA stated, "Physician-assisted suicide is fundamentally incompatible with the physician's role as healer, would be difficult or impossible to control, and would pose serious societal risks." The goal of medicine is to heal and to cure and, where that is not possible, to comfort the patient. Doctors are expected to act always in the best interests of the patient. Dr. Leon Kass, former chair of the President's Council on Bioethics, asks the following common sense question: "Will doctors be able to care wholeheartedly for patients when it is always possible to think of killing them as a 'therapeutic option?'" In Holland, reports have been published documenting the sad fact that elderly patients, out of fear of euthanasia, refuse hospitalization and even avoid consulting doctors. Dutch citizens have begun to fear that their doctors, instead of being caregivers, will become their executioners.

We Must Choose More Life, Not More Death

It could lead to a devaluing of human life: [As the US Council of Catholic Bishops states in "To Live Each Day with Dignity,"]

> Taking life in the name of compassion also invites a slippery slope toward ending the lives of people with non-terminal conditions. Dutch doctors, who once limited euthanasia to terminally ill patients, now provide lethal drugs to people with chronic illnesses and disabilities, mental illness, and even melancholy. Once they convinced themselves that ending a short life can be an act of compassion, it was morbidly logical to conclude that ending a longer life may show even more compassion. Psychologically, as well, the physician who has begun to offer death as a solution for some illnesses is tempted to view it as the answer for an ever-broader range of problems.

It could lead to an increase of suicide generally: Oregon, the first state to legalize physician-assisted suicide, has one of the highest rates of suicide (not including deaths from PAS) of any state in the nation. It begs a logical question: How can a state effectively both try to minimize suicide in some situations and promote it as a legal alternative in other situations? Is it reasonable to expect that efforts to prevent suicides will be undermined by legalizing suicide and presenting it as normal and acceptable for those with terminal diagnoses?

What Legalized Assisted Suicide Looks Like

It could lead, eventually, to euthanasia—like it has in the Netherlands: It is very sobering to see the evolution of physician-assisted suicide in the Netherlands [NL], a modern industrialized country. In 1973 the "Right to Die—NL" was founded and euthanasia has been legal in the Netherlands for more than a decade. The *New York Times* reported in their April 3, 2012, edition that "Right to Die—NL" is campaigning for expanded euthanasia, in the form of mobile teams to go out to people's homes to euthanize them. They are also promoting the idea that euthanasia should no longer be limited just to the terminally ill, and their proposal envisions the service for any individual over 70 years of age who requests it.

The Dutch patients' organization, NPV, strongly criticizes the current application of the law, saying the practice of euthanasia

Physician-Assisted Suicide in the United States

As of 2014, just three states—Oregon, Washington, and Vermont—had legalized physician assisted suicide. Attempts to legalize it have failed in California, Connecticut, Maine, Massachusetts, Michigan, and many other states, in part because voters were not convinced it would not lead to abuse and coercion.

States with legal and active assisted suicide program

Taken from: Patients Rights Council, 2013.

has been extended to include patients with dementia and other conditions who may not, by definition, be competent to request help in dying, including children. Elise Van Hock-Burgerhart, a spokeswoman for NPV, told the *New York Times* reporter that the idea of mobile euthanasia teams was a matter of concern because there was no way for the mobile team doctors to get to know the patients. Moreover, she stated that research in the Netherlands indicated that requests for euthanasia from the elderly would be substantially reduced if palliative care were better in their country and that the country should be working toward improving palliative care, not increasing euthanasia. She also indicated that the law in the Netherlands required review committees to sign off on every reported case of euthanasia, but that 469 cases from 2010 had still not been reviewed; 2010 is the latest year for which data is available. That year 3,136 notifications of termination of life on request were reported, indicating that it was not clear how well doctors were adhering to the official guidelines. Anyone that believes that a "slippery slope" doesn't exist with assisted suicide and euthanasia only has to look at its "evolution" in the Netherlands.

Legalized Physician-Assisted Suicide Has Many Safeguards to Prevent Abuse and Coerced Death

Marcia Angell

Legalized physician-assisted suicide will not result in coerced death, argues Marcia Angell in the following viewpoint. She contends that in places where physician-assisted suicide is legal, it has not resulted in increased suicide rates, elder abuse, or other nefarious acts. Rather, it has helped terminally ill people feel as in control regarding their deaths as they felt about their lives. This is psychologically and spiritually important, says Angell—suffering from a terminal disease leaves many people feeling humiliated, dysfunctional, and in terrible pain at the end of their lives. Few want to be remembered this way—they would rather choose the time and manner of their death so they can end their lives with dignity and pride. Angell maintains that the law should allow them to do this because it has built-in safeguards that prevent abuse.

Angell lectures on social medicine at Harvard Medical School and formerly served as editor in chief of the *New England Journal of Medicine*.

Marcia Angell, "A Method for Dying with Dignity," *Boston Globe*, September 29, 2012.

On Nov. 6, [2012,] Massachusetts voters will decide whether physicians may provide a dying patient, whose suffering has become unbearable, with medication to bring about an earlier, more peaceful death if the patient chooses and the physician agrees. On the ballot will be a Death with Dignity Act—Question 2—that is virtually identical to the law that has been in effect in Oregon for nearly 15 years. [Editor's note: The Massachusetts voters rejected the proposition.]

When Life Becomes Meaningless

Good palliative care is adequate for the great majority of dying patients, but not all. Most pain can be eased, but other symptoms are harder to deal with—weakness, loss of control of bodily functions,

Despite the fact that physician-assisted suicide is legal in Oregon, in 2011 the state's legislators banned the sale of so-called suicide kits (shown) that are meant to be used by individuals to kill themselves.

Safeguards Against Abuse

Since Oregon's Death with Dignity Act (DWDA) went into effect in 1997, only 1,050 lethal prescriptions have been written, resulting in 673 deaths. Supporters say the many safeguards built into law prevent physician-assisted suicide from being abused.

Death with Dignity Act Prescription Recipients and Deaths, by Year, Oregon

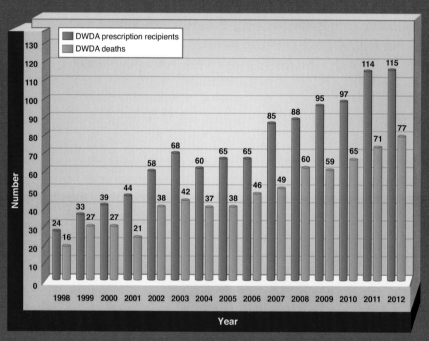

Taken from: "Oregon's Death with Dignity Act—2012." Oregon Public Health Division, January 2013.

shortness of breath, and nausea—and the drugs to treat these symptoms often produce unacceptable side effects. Even worse for many dying patients is the existential suffering. They know their condition is inexorably downhill, and they find it meaningless to soldier on.

This is not a matter of life versus death, but about the timing and manner of an inevitable death. That is why many prefer the term "physician-assisted dying" to "physician-assisted suicide." In the usual suicide someone with a normal life expectancy chooses death over life. Terminally ill patients don't have that choice.

Many Safeguards Prevent Abuse

Like the Oregon law, Question 2 contains a host of safeguards. It applies only to adults able to make their own decisions, and the patient must be capable of swallowing the medication—usually barbiturates dissolved in a full glass of liquid—which helps ensure that it is voluntary. Euthanasia (the injection of a lethal medication) is not permitted. The patient must have a terminal illness, with a life expectancy of no more than six months, as determined by at least two physicians.

The patient is to make two oral requests for the medication, separated by at least 15 days, and one written request, with two witnesses. If a physician believes a psychological condition is impairing the patient's judgment, the physician must refer the patient to a psychiatrist or other licensed counselor. No physician is required to participate; they may refuse for any reason whatsoever. This is a choice for both patients and physicians.

Assisted Suicide Works Where It Is Legal

Nearly everyone knows someone who has wished for an earlier death while suffering from a terminal illness, and polls show that most people believe physicians should be able to help such patients die. But we are now being barraged by warnings that the Death with Dignity Act will put us on an ethical "slippery slope" leading to the widespread coercion of vulnerable patients to end their lives, even when they may not be dying and their suffering could be relieved.

The best answers come from Oregon. Assisted dying there has accounted for 596 deaths over the past 14 years [from 1997 to 2011], only 0.2 percent of all deaths in the most recent year [2012].

Most of these patients were suffering from disseminated [spread throughout the body] cancer, and the prognosis was clear. Far from being vulnerable, they were relatively affluent, well-educated, and well-insured, and nearly all were receiving good hospice care. They were no more likely to be depressed than other dying patients, and there was no evidence of coercion by unscrupulous families. About a third of patients who received medication didn't use it, but kept it at hand for peace of mind. No law works absolutely perfectly, but this one comes about as close as possible.

People Should Be Able to Die with Dignity

Unfortunately, the Massachusetts Medical Society officially opposes the Act because it believes it is "inconsistent with the physician's role as healer," in the words of its past president. But this isn't about physicians or their self-image; it's about patients—specifically patients for whom healing is no longer possible. They, not physicians, are the ones to say when their suffering is no longer bearable, and individual physicians (many of whom disagree with the position of the medical society) should be able to honor their wishes. Why should anyone—the state, the medical profession or anyone else—presume to tell someone how much suffering they must endure as their life is ending? We respect people's right to self-determination when they're healthy. That shouldn't be denied to them when they're dying.

NINE

Hospice Care Is Preferable to Assisted Suicide

Linda Campanella

Hospice care is end-of-life care in which dying patients are kept comfortable until they die naturally. In the following viewpoint Linda Campanella argues that hospice care offers the dying a compassionate, dignified way to exit this world, and thus should be emphasized over measures to legalize physician-assisted suicide. She recounts her own mother's experience with hospice care, saying it afforded her mother the time she needed to end her life in a joyful, peaceful, and dignified way. Campanella suggests that physician-assisted suicide skips over this important transitional experience, robbing both the dying and their families of important last months together. Rather than seeking to legalize assisted suicide, she concludes that states should do more to improve and expand hospice care.

Campanella is the author of the book *When All That's Left of Me Is Love: A Daughter's Story of Letting Go.*

A bill before the Connecticut General Assembly would legalize physician-assisted suicide [which was defeated at the polls in 2013]: The legislature's debate about dying patients' rights should focus instead, or at least in addition, on their right

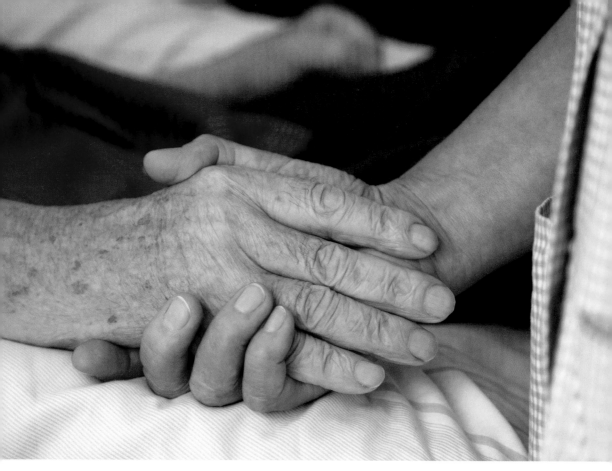

Hospice care offers the dying a compassionate, dignified way to exit this world and should be preferred over physician-assisted suicide, argues the author.

to receive compassionate care. Assuming the underlying goal is to reduce the suffering of terminally ill people, then promoting quality-of-life care rather than passing right-to-die legislation is a better strategy. The number of people who stand to benefit is exponentially larger.

A Loving, Peaceful Death

My terminally ill mother received compassionate care that made the unbearable bearable—for her and for the family that already was grieving her loss. For three months, a hospice team surrounded us with love and comfort.

Even in her final weeks, my dying mother woke up every morning looking forward to the living still to do. She fell asleep every night feeling grateful. She died with dignity and without pain—physical or emotional. Her caregivers understood that suffering is not just a physical phenomenon caused by symptoms of disease and pain; suffering is also caused by the existential distress people feel when experiencing anxiety, fear, loss of hope, loss of control.

The medications provided by our hospice nurse, in close consultation with Mom's primary care doctor, took care of the physical pain. The greater gift, however, was the relief my mother received from her emotional suffering—relief from the guilt she felt over having become, she believed, a burden to her family; relief from the fear she experienced when she imagined being without her family in whatever state or place she would be in after death; relief from the sadness and anxiety that gripped her when she realized she would not be here to take care of her beloved husband of 52 years.

When she died, she and those she left behind were at peace. We all were grateful. None of us had regrets.

Care for the Body, Mind, and Soul

Hospice provided compassionate, competent care for my mother's whole person—her body, her mind, her soul—and for her whole family. Too few people understand what hospice is, and too many believe it is something it isn't. Sometimes people—both physicians and families—wait too long to bring in hospice. A family that waits until a loved one is on the verge of his or her last breath is missing out on a wonderful experience. I never could have imagined just how wonderful, and might still struggle to believe it possible at all, had I not experienced the gift of hospice firsthand.

We need to talk more about death and dying. The topic should not be so taboo. We need to raise awareness about quality-of-life medicine, for body and soul, as an essential element of end-of-life care. Doctors should not think of death as a failure. When healing and cures are not possible, we need not consider the situation "hopeless." Rather, we should redefine and redirect hope in the way hospice defines and nurtures it—hope that remaining days will be lived with as much joy and dignity, and as little physical or emotional pain, as possible.

Focus on Compassionate Care Rather than on Death

My mother, who received her terminal diagnosis on Sept. 8, 2008, and died a year and a day later, wanted to live, love and laugh until she took her last breath. So her four children and husband

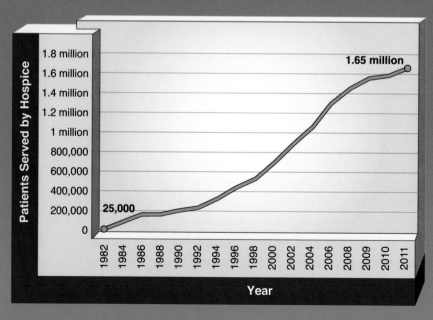

Hospice Care Is on the Rise

The number of patients served by hospice facilities has vastly increased over thirty years, as has the number of facilities.

Patients Served by Hospice in the United States, 1982 to 2011

did everything we could to help her live fully and joyfully (and she did, till the end), and then we gave her what a close friend of mine termed a good death. Hospice helped her, and helped us, achieve what we hoped for.

This was, one might say, assisted dying as opposed to assisted suicide.

So as assisted suicide starts grabbing headlines and our attention, can we also celebrate hospice and draw attention to the compassionate, quality-of-life care that is already and readily available for the dying? Can we shine the light on the inspiring people and organizations advocating for a sharper focus on the "care" in health care and trying to establish palliative care as an academic discipline in medical schools, as a medical subspecialty for practicing physicians and as an option available in most, if not all, our nation's hospitals?

TEN

Hospice Care Is Not Preferable to Assisted Suicide

John M. Crisp

Hospice care prolongs death in an undignified and painful way, argues John Crisp in the following viewpoint. He says physician-assisted suicide—in which doctors are legally allowed to prescribe a lethal dose of medication to terminally ill patients—offers the dying a better end to life. Crisp describes his uncle's swift death, saying that an accident that broke the man's skull mercifully saved him from the months of prolonged discomfort, disability, and indignity that he otherwise would have experienced in hospice care. In Crisp's opinion, hospice care forces one to slip away in a cruel, gradual way; assisted suicide, on the other hand, allows the terminally ill to determine when their life is no longer worth living. Assisted suicide is routinely viewed as humane and appropriate for pets and killers who are executed by the state; Crisp concludes the same compassion should be extended to all Americans.

Crisp teaches English at Del Mar College in Corpus Christi, Texas.

My uncle got a lucky break last week—literally. He got up in the middle of the night and, enfeebled at 81 years of age, he fell, hitting his head on a desk and breaking his skull. Later the next night he died, having never regained consciousness.

Spared the Agony of Hospice

Why am I calling this gruesome mishap lucky? Because a few months earlier he had been diagnosed with lung cancer, and a couple of days before he died he had gone into hospice care. He was facing several months of increasing discomfort, disability and undignified decline, and then real pain and finally a smothering death. With a misstep in the middle of the night, he managed to avoid all of that.

Barbara Wise wasn't quite so "lucky." She suffered a stroke recently and was bedridden in a Cleveland hospital, unable to move or speak. John Wise, her husband of 45 years, smuggled a pistol into her hospital room and fired a single round into her head. She died the next day. Even though Wise and his wife had agreed long ago that neither of them wished to live in a bedridden, disabled state, prosecutors have charged the 66-year-old Wise with aggravated murder.

An Associated Press story reports that some authorities believe that the Wises' unhappy circumstances will become more and more common as baby boomers age and as medical technology continues to advance in its capacity to keep alive, in whatever condition, patients who would have died quickly only a few years ago.

Quality of Life Is More Important than Life Itself

Maybe this is a good problem to have; nearly everyone wants to live longer.

But as a nation, we are probably unprepared for the financial burden presented by more and more sick people who live longer, the psychological burden that caregivers will have to bear and the legal burden that will ensue when caregivers like John Wise take matters into their own hands.

All of these issues call for careful consideration, but the real heart of this problem—the issue that needs enlightened scrutiny—is the tenacity with which we cling to life, no matter how much its quality has declined.

John Wise (pictured) was charged with aggravated murder after killing his sixty-five-year-old terminally ill wife in her hospital bed even though his wife had agreed he should take her life.

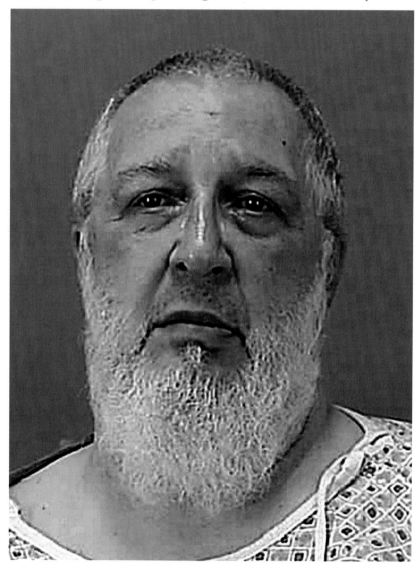

Some Hospice Stays Are Very Long

Although many people are in hospice for a week or less before their death, more than a third spend several months.

Proportion of Patients by Length of Service, 2011

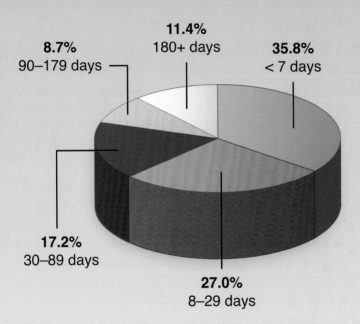

11.4%
180+ days

8.7%
90–179 days

35.8%
< 7 days

17.2%
30–89 days

27.0%
8–29 days

Taken from: National Hospice and Palliative Care Organization. "Hospice Care in America," 2012.

No one who's alive and healthy can speak with much authority about the decisions that the gravely ill face at the ends of their lives. Still, it doesn't take much imagination to understand a little of the desperation that caregivers like John Wise must feel when their loved ones reach miserable, persistent conditions, from which the only escape is death.

We like to imagine death as a peaceful, serene passage, like we see in the movies. But considerable evidence indicates that, more often than not, death is miserable, painful, prolonged and undignified.

A Good Death Is Swift and Gentle

But philosophy and religion, rather than medicine, stand in the way of a gentler, more humane death. Some countries, like Switzerland, permit active suicide assistance for terminal patients, but in the U.S. only three states—Washington, Oregon and Montana—have developed laws that allow versions of physician-assisted suicide, under highly controlled conditions.

In the face of laws against assisted suicide in most other states, terminal patients occasionally benefit from kindly nurses and doctors who are willing to supply enough morphine and other drugs to significantly ease, and sometimes hasten, the passage into the Great Beyond.

But many others aren't so lucky, and they suffer greatly from the obligation—self-imposed or imposed by others—to let nature or God's will take its course despite whatever prolonged suffering and misery it might entail.

Of course, everyone who wants to die that way should have the option, and it's presumptuous of us to tell others when and how they should let go of life.

But perhaps it's time to alleviate the stigma that prevents us from easing our deaths as much as possible and to provide for ourselves the legal option of a passage as gentle as the ones we insist on for our pets and for serial killers.

ELEVEN

It Is Never Moral to End the Lives of Children

Andrew Brown

In the following viewpoint Andrew Brown argues it is never acceptable to end the lives of children. He opposes a suggestion by ethicists Alberto Giubilini and Francesca Minerva that newborn children be killed if they are born exhibiting the same kinds of diseases that parents would abort a fetus for. Brown is offended by the ethicists' suggestions that newborns are not full persons and have no right to life. No matter what one's position on abortion is, Brown thinks all people should be repelled by the suggestion that it is ever ethical to kill a child once it is born.

Writer and editor Brown is a frequent contributor to the British newspaper the *Guardian*.

If you write an article proposing that newborn babies be killed, many people will find you morally disgusting. This should be obvious even to a professional philosopher. Yet Julian Savulescu, the editor of the British Medical Journal's *Journal of Medical Ethics*, who published such an article, appears outraged himself at the reaction it has provoked.

An Offensive and Immoral Suggestion

The latest issue of the journal carries an article by Alberto Giubilini and Francesca Minerva, two ethicists at Melbourne University in Australia, arguing that we should accept the killing of newborn infants for any of the reasons that we now accept as justifying abortion. There need be nothing wrong with the infant to justify its death. It is enough that its life should inconvenience the parents.

"We claim that killing a newborn could be ethically permissible in all the circumstances where abortion would be," write Giubilini and Minerva. "Such circumstances include cases where the newborn has the potential to have an (at least) acceptable life, but the well-being of the family is at risk. Accordingly, a second terminological specification is that we call such a practice 'after-birth abortion' rather than 'euthanasia' because the best interest of the one who dies is not necessarily the primary criterion for the choice, contrary to what happens in the case of euthanasia."

The argument by which they reach this position hinges on the idea that neither a fetus nor a newborn is a real person. An "actual person" in their terms is someone who can have plans and aims. As such, they are wronged by being killed if this deprives them of the chance to carry out their plans. But a newborn is incapable of planning, or having aims, just as a fetus is. Therefore, they say, it is only a "potential person" and, though pain can harm it, death can not.

Newborns Are Most Definitely Persons

In this line of reasoning, only the parents are harmed by the death of a newborn, because their plans and aims may be frustrated. But "potential persons" can't be harmed that way: "If you ask one of us if we would have been harmed, had our parents decided to kill us when we were fetuses or newborns, our answer is 'no', because they would have harmed someone who does not exist (the 'us' whom you are asking the question), which means no one. And if no one is harmed, then no harm occurred."

This reasoning impressed Savulescu greatly. In his defence of the paper on his blog, he wrote:

> The novel contribution of this paper is not an argument in favour of infanticide—the paper repeats the arguments made famous by [ethicists Michael] Tooley and [Peter] Singer—but rather their application in consideration of maternal and family interests.
>
> The authors provocatively argue that there is no moral difference between a fetus and a newborn. Their capacities are relevantly similar. If abortion is permissible, infanticide should be permissible. The authors proceed logically from premises which many people accept to a conclusion that many of those people would reject.

Some modern utilitarian philosophers have argued that there is no huge moral difference between a baby about to be born, at the top of the birth canal, and the same baby when it has emerged into the world. I first heard this from John Harris, at Manchester University. But the conclusion he drew was not that we ought to kill newborns.

Abortion's Moral Limit

The equation of abortion with infanticide is central to the rhetoric of many anti-abortionists. It is something that most pro-choicers emphatically reject. For them, the moral justification of abortion lies in the fact that an embryo is not a human being, whereas a newborn baby is. The moral status of a fetus changes over time in the womb, and while there will always be arguments about when the change should be recognised, there is wide agreement that a time limit on abortion is morally significant.

It certainly seems to follow from Giubilini and Minerva's reasoning that there is nothing wrong with sex-selective infanticide. There's no doubt that having a child of the wrong sex can be frightfully inconvenient for its parents. So if it's all right to abort a girl for her chromosomes, why not kill the newborns as well?

This question is not addressed in the article.

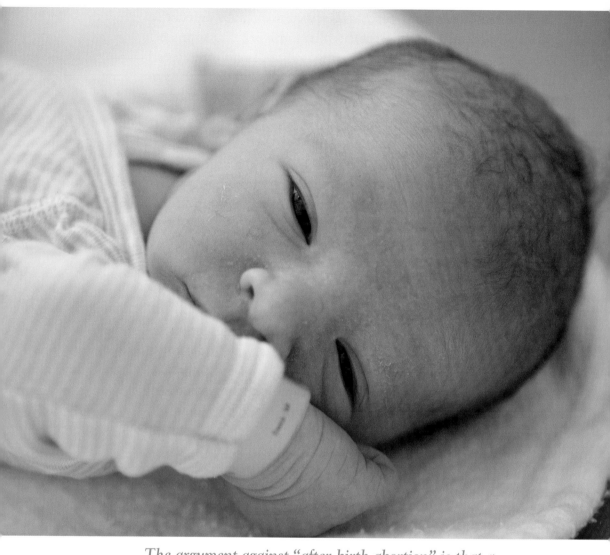

The argument against "after-birth abortion" is that a newborn is a person and not the same as a fetus.

We Should Be Repelled by Such Monstrosity

In any case, the piece was picked up by the website of the immensely popular rightwing American Mormon, Glenn Beck. The commentators there—who probably already believe that there is no difference between abortion and infanticide, or believe that they believe this—erupted in predictable fury.

Savulescu claims that he and the authors have received death threats. In his blogpost he wrote: "What is disturbing is not the arguments in this paper nor its publication in an ethics journal. It is the hostile, abusive, threatening responses that it has elicited. More than ever, proper academic discussion and freedom are under threat from fanatics opposed to the very values of a liberal society."

You have to wonder whether this is intended as self-parody.

If "the very values of a liberal society" include killing inconvenient babies, or discussing their killing as if this was something reasonable and morally competent human beings might choose to do, then liberalism really would be the monster that American conservatives pretend it is. Academics are and should be free to entertain monstrous ideas. But that does not trump the freedom of the rest of us to be repelled by their monstrosity.

TWELVE

Technology May Allow Humans to Live Forever

Ray Kurzweil, as told to Duncan Begg

> Ray Kurzweil is a futurist and the author of the book *Transcend—Nine Steps to Living Well Forever*. In the following viewpoint he argues in an interview with reporter Duncan Begg from the British tabloid the *Sun* that technology will eventually enable humans to infinitely extend their lifespans. Already, technological breakthroughs have allowed humans to do more than was capable just a few decades ago, asserts Kurzweil. In the future, he predicts, humans will be outfitted with devices that combat disease, extend their mental capacity, and otherwise help the body work more efficiently and powerfully. He envisions a world in which human life is threatened only by an accident, such as being hit by a bus or suffering a catastrophic fall. Kurzweil concludes that technological advances will remove the limits on human life in amazing and historic ways.

We are living through the most exciting period of human history.

Computer technology and our understanding of genes—our body's software programs—are accelerating at an incredible rate.

I and many other scientists now believe that in around 20 years we will have the means to reprogramme our bodies' stone-age software so we can halt, then reverse, ageing. Then nanotechnology will let us live for ever.

Technology Will Combat Disease

Already, blood cell–sized submarines called nanobots are being tested in animals. These will soon be used to destroy tumours, unblock clots and perform operations without scars.

Ultimately, nanobots will replace blood cells and do their work thousands of times more effectively.

Within 25 years we will be able to do an Olympic sprint for 15 minutes without taking a breath, or go scuba-diving for four hours without oxygen.

Heart-attack victims—who haven't taken advantage of widely available bionic hearts—will calmly drive to the doctors for a minor operation as their blood bots keep them alive.

Nanotechnology will extend our mental capacities to such an extent we will be able to write books within minutes.

A Billion-Fold Increase in What We Can Do

If we want to go into virtual-reality mode, nanobots will shut down brain signals and take us wherever we want to go. Virtual sex will become commonplace. And in our daily lives, hologram-like figures will pop up in our brain to explain what is happening.

These technologies should not seem at all fanciful. Our phones now perform tasks we wouldn't have dreamed possible 20 years ago. When I was a student in 1965, my university's only computer cost £7million and was huge.

Today your mobile phone is a million times less expensive and a thousand times more powerful. That's a billion times more capable for the same price.

According to my theory—the Law of Accelerating Returns— we will experience another billion-fold increase in technological capability for the same cost in the next 25 years.

The Path to Immortality

So we can look forward to a world where humans become cyborgs, with artificial limbs and organs.

This might sound far-fetched, but remember, diabetics already have artificial pancreases and Parkinson's patients have neural implants.

Computer artwork depicts a medical nanobot, a microscopic robot with a wide range of medical uses.

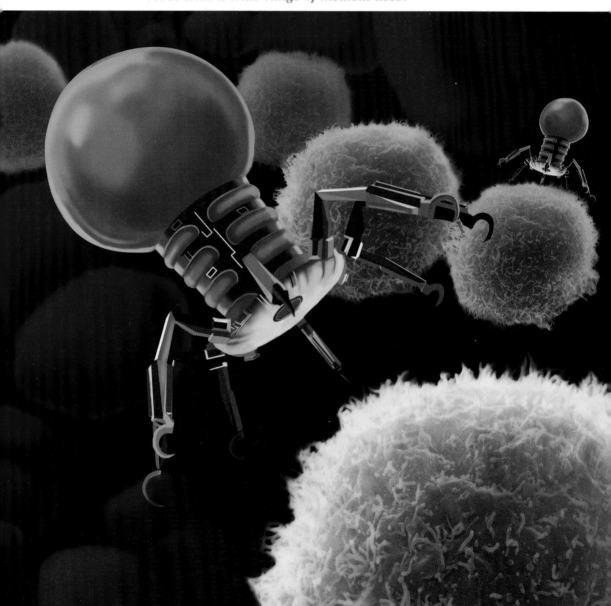

As we approach the 21st century's second decade, stunning medical breakthroughs are a regular occurrence.

In 2008 we discovered skin cells can be transformed into the equivalent of embryonic cells. So organs will soon be repaired and eventually grown.

In a few years most people will have their entire genetic sequences mapped. Before long, we will all know the diseases we are susceptible to and gene therapies will mean virtually no genetic problems that can't be erased.

It's important to ensure we get to take advantage of the upcoming technologies by living well and not getting hit by a bus.

By the middle of this century we will have back-up copies of the information in our bodies and brains that make us who we are. Then we really will be immortal.

What You Should Know About Death and Dying

Facts About Hospice and Palliative Care

The National Hospice and Palliative Care Organization asserts the following facts:

- In 2011 an estimated 1.651 million patients received hospice services.
- Approximately 44.6 percent of all deaths in the United States occur under the care of a hospice program.
- The median length of stay in hospice was 19.1 days. This means that half of all hospice patients received care for less than three weeks and half received care for more than three weeks.
- The average length of service was 69.1 days.
- Approximately 35.7 percent of hospice patients died or were discharged within seven days of admission.
- Hospice patients 65 years of age or older make up 83.3 percent of hospice users.
- More than one-third of all hospice patients were 85 years of age or older.
- The pediatric and young adult population accounted for less than 1 percent of hospice admissions. The specific age breakdown was:
  - younger than 24 years: 0.4 percent;
  - 25–34 years old: 0.4 percent;
  - 35–64 years old: 16 percent;

- 65–74 years old: 16.3 percent;
- 75–84 years old: 27.6 percent were;
- 85 or older: 39.3 percent were.
- Those of non-Hispanic origin composed 93.8 percent of hospice patients whereas
- 6.2 percent were of Hispanic or Latino origin. More specific racial/ethnic breakdowns were as follows:
  - white/Caucasian: 82.8 percent;
  - multiracial or another race: 6.1 percent;
  - Black/African American: 8.5 percent;
  - Asian, Hawaiian, or other Pacific Islander: 2.4 percent;
  - American Indian or Alaska Native: 0.2 percent.
- Of these patients, 37.7 percent had a primary diagnosis of cancer;
- 62.3 percent had a noncancer diagnosis. Of these:
  - 13.9 percent had an unspecified diagnosis;
  - 12.5 percent had dementia;
  - 11.4 percent had heart disease;
  - 8.5 percent had lung disease;
  - 4.8 percent had another kind of disease;
  - 4.1 percent had a stroke or were in a coma;
  - 2.7 percent had kidney disease;
  - 2.1 percent had liver disease;
  - 1.6 percent had non-ALS (amyotrophic lateral sclerosis) motor neuron disease.

Facts About Physician-Assisted Suicide in the United States

As of 2013 physician-assisted suicide was legal and accessible in three American states:

- Oregon (legalized in 1994, went into effect in 1997)
- Washington (legalized in 2008, went into effect in 2009)
- Vermont (legalized in 2013)

In 2009 the Montana Supreme Court cleared the way to legalize physician-assisted suicide, but the practice is on hold pending further appeals and court rulings.

The Oregon Public Health Division, the Washington Department of Health, and the Vermont Department of Health have very similar requirements for eligibility and participation in their programs. To be eligible to obtain a lethal prescription, a person must

- legally reside in the state offering the option;
- be eighteen years of age or older;
- be capable of making and communicating health care decisions for him/herself;
- be diagnosed with a terminal illness;
- have six months or less to live; and
- have two physicians independently assess whether these criteria have been met.

Patients must complete the following procedure:

- orally request a lethal prescription from their physicians;
- wait fifteen days, then make a second oral request to their physicians;
- make a written request to their physicians;
- wait forty-eight hours before picking up their prescribed medications; and
- pick up prescribed medications from a pharmacy.

To prevent abuse, coercion, hasty deaths, or deaths due to depression, these states' Death with Dignity Acts (DWDAs) include the following safeguards:

- The patient must be able to self-administer and ingest the prescribed medication—no other party is allowed to administer it to them.
- Patient must separate his or her requests for lethal medication by at least fifteen days.
- The written request that follows the oral requests must be witnessed by two individuals who are neither primary care givers nor family members.
- The patient can rescind the verbal and written requests at any time.

- The attending physician must be licensed in the same state that the requesting patient resides in.
- The patient's diagnosis (which must include a terminal illness and less than six months to live) must be certified by a consulting physician, who must also certify that the patient is mentally competent to make and communicate health care decisions.
- If either physician determines that the patient's judgment is impaired, the patient must be referred for a psychological examination.
- The attending physician must inform the patient of alternatives, including palliative care, hospice, and pain management options.
- The attending physician must request that the patient notify next of kin of the prescription request.
- Use of the law cannot affect the status of a patient's health insurance or life insurance policies.

These states' laws ban the following practices:

- involuntary euthanasia/mercy killing (in which a patient's death is caused without the patient's consent)
- active euthanasia (in which a medical professional or layperson directly administers a lethal substance to the patient).

According to the Oregon Public Health Division, in Oregon as of 2013,

- a total of 1,050 people have had lethal prescriptions written for them since the Death with Dignity Act went into effect in 1997;
- of these, 673 patients have died from ingesting the prescribed medications;
- in 2012 prescriptions for lethal medications were written for 115 people; of these:
    - 67 people (58.3 percent) ingested the medication,
    - 66 people died from ingesting the medication (one patient ingested the medication but regained consciousness before dying of the original illness,

- 23 people did not take the medications and subsequently died of other causes, and
  - ingestion status was unknown for 25 patients.
- Of the seventy-seven DWDA deaths that occurred during 2012, most (67.5 percent) of the decedents were aged sixty-five years or older, 97.4 percent were white, 42.9 percent were well educated, 75.3 percent had cancer, and 97.4 percent died at home.
- Ninety-seven percent were enrolled in hospice care either at the time the DWDA prescription was written or at the time of death,
- 100 percent had some form of health insurance,
- 93.5 percent stated their primary end-of-life concerns included loss of autonomy,
- 92.2 percent stated their primary end-of-life concerns included decreasing ability to participate in activities that made life enjoyable, and
- 77.9 percent stated that their primary end-of-life concerns included a fear of losing their dignity.
- Sixty-one physicians wrote the 115 prescriptions provided during 2012.
- In 2012 zero referrals were made to the Oregon Medical Board for failure to comply with DWDA requirements.

According to the Washington Department of Health, in Washington in 2012,

- Lethal medication was dispensed to 121 individuals.
- Prescriptions were written by eighty-seven different physicians.
- Medications were dispensed by thirty different pharmacists.
- Of the 121 participants in 2012,
  - 104 are known to have died;
  - 83 died after ingesting the medication, and
  - 18 died without having ingested the medication.
  - For the remaining 3 people who died, ingestion status was unknown.
  - For the remaining 17 people, no documentation was received that indicated death had occurred.

- The 104 people who died ranged in age from 35 to 95 years old.
- Of the 104 who died,
  - 73 percent had cancer;
  - 10 percent had neurodegenerative disease, including ALS;
  - 17 percent had other illnesses, including heart and respiratory disease;
  - 97 percent of those who died were white, non-Hispanics, 43 percent were married, and 82 percent had at least some college education;
  - 94 percent reported to their health care provider concerns about loss of autonomy;
  - 84 percent reported to their health care provider concerns about loss of dignity;
  - 90 percent reported to their health care provider concerns about loss of the ability to participate in activities that make life enjoyable.
- Of the 83 participants in 2012 who died after ingesting the medication,
  - 89 percent were at home at the time of death, and
  - 92 percent were enrolled in hospice care when they ingested the medication.

Facts About the Cost of End-of-Life Care

- CNN.com estimates that one out of every four Medicare dollars—more than $125 billion—is spent on services for 5 percent of beneficiaries in their last year of life.
- According to a 2012 study funded by the National Institute on Aging and conducted with Mount Sinai School of Medicine,
  - The average Medicare benefit recipient paid $38,688 for medical expenses in the last five years of life, which included the cost of hiring at-home caregivers and other long-term care expenses.
  - The top quarter of Medicare recipients averaged costs of $101,791.

- The bottom quartile averaged costs of $5,163.
- Seniors with dementia or Alzheimer's disease spent the most for health care—about $66,000—which was more than twice that of patients with gastrointestinal disease or cancer, who spent an average of $31,000.
- A study published in 2009 by the National Institutes of Health comparing costs of care during the last week of life found that
  - patients that discussed end-of-life care with their health care providers had $1,876 in care costs during the last week of life;
  - patients that did not discuss end-of-life care with their health care providers had $2,917 in care costs during the last week of life;
  - patients with higher costs had lower quality of death; and
  - advanced cancer patients who reported having end-of-life conversations with their health care providers had significantly lower health care costs in their final week of life.
- A 2013 report issued by the Dartmouth Institute for Health Policy & Clinical Practice found that the national average amount that Medicare spent on chronically ill patients during the last two years of life was $69,947; this was a 15.2 percent increase from the $60,694 spent in 2007.
- According to a 2012 analysis of Medicare benefit recipients undertaken by the *Wall Street Journal*,
  - the top 10 percent of Medicare beneficiaries who received hospital care accounted for 64 percent of the program's hospital spending;
  - Medicare patients racked up disproportionate costs in the final year of life; and
  - 6.6 percent (1.6 million) of the Medicare patients who received hospital care died, and these accounted for 22.3 percent of total hospital expenditures.

What You Should Do About Death and Dying

A fact of life is that everyone dies; less certain is how, when, and under what circumstances. Although every American will surely reach the end of their lives, few are prepared for this day and understandably so: Death is scary, intangible, and for most people, seems like something that will not happen anytime soon.

But being unprepared for death is one of the things that makes it so controversial. In fact, many of the controversies related to death and dying involve the high cost of end-of-life care and the very personal and sensitive decisions that need to be made, often on behalf of others who can no longer communicate their wishes. In many cases these costs and decisions are made more stressful, and more expensive, because people have not planned for the moment that inevitably comes to all of us.

Lack of end-of-life planning accounts for much of the high costs associated with death. The National Institutes of Health estimates that people who discuss end-of-life care in advance of their deaths pay about 36 percent less for care during their last week of life than do people who do not have this discussion. Failure to create an end-of-life care plan can rack up tens of thousands of dollars or more over the course of weeks or months. Lack of end-of-life planning can cause costs to spiral because relatives tend to be more aggressive about treatment than patients themselves would be. But because many such patients do not discuss their preferences for end-of-life care in advance of a serious illness, accident, or other terminal situation, their relatives are left only to guess at their wishes. For example, according to the Pew Research Center, although 100 percent of Americans will die, only 29 percent have a living will, despite the fact that 71 percent of Americans have thought about end-of-life treatment preferences and 95 percent have heard of a living will. Therefore, discussing end-of-life care in advance of terminal illness can be one of the most important financial and personal conversations a family can have.

Discuss End-of-Life Care Preferences with the People You Love

Broaching the topic of death and dying is no easy feat. People close to death have trouble facing the fact that they are in the last stages of life, while people seemingly far from death feel it is too far off to be of imminent concern. Therefore, you will likely need to convince the people with whom you speak that discussing the end of life is an uncomfortable yet necessary conversation, and one that comes from a place of love.

First, you will need to identify people in your life whose end-of-life care or death might personally affect you. Do you have grand-parents, parents, stepparents, aunts, uncles, cousins, siblings, or other loved ones who might rely on you to provide critical levels of care? Do you have family members who might defer to you to make medical decisions in the event they become unable to communicate their wishes? Might you become financially responsible for anyone's medical bills? Or, even if you would not be directly financially or practically responsible for anyone in such a situation, do you know people who should consider these difficult issues, for the entire family's peace of mind? Make a list of people in your life who may fit these criteria.

Once you know with whom you want to speak, you will need to let the person know you would like to have a sensitive, but important, conversation. Raising the topic may be the most difficult part. You can say something like, "I'd like to discuss what our plan should be if you get really sick, or even terminally ill. Can we do that?" Or, "I'm afraid of not knowing what to do in the event you get very sick or hurt. It would make me feel better to know we have a plan in place. Can we take some time to create one?" Or simply, "What should I do if you suddenly need long-term care?"

Once they agree to talk, select a time, choose a quiet, distraction-free setting, and bring a notepad or laptop on which to take notes. Some key questions to ask include:

- If you were diagnosed with a terminal illness, what types of treatment would you prefer?
- How invasive or extensive would you like such care to be?
- Are there certain medical treatments that you would particularly want? (Examples might include chemotherapy, surgery, dialysis, biopsy, etc.) Are there certain treatments that you particularly fear or know you do not want? (Examples might include resuscitation, feeding tubes, breathing or life support, etc.)
- Would you want to be resuscitated if you stop breathing and/or your heart stops?
- Would you want doctors to do everything possible to save your life?
- Would cost be an issue for you in your care?
- Is it more important to you that you make every effort to cure your condition, or that you die quickly and easily?
- Have you selected someone to make medical and financial decisions for you in the event you become unable to do so?
- Do you have an advance directive? If so, where is it and what does it generally include?
- Do you have a living will? If so, where is it and what does it generally include?
- If you have not created an advance directive, living will, or other document related to end-of-life planning, what has prevented you from doing so? Is there something you fear? Do you think it unnecessary? When do you plan on doing so?
- Do you have a do-not-resuscitate order? Why or why not?
- If you were seriously or terminally ill, where would you like to be cared for? At home? In a nursing facility? In hospice care? Somewhere else?
- In the event you need serious and/or long-term care, how do you imagine this care will be paid for? Do you have insurance? What kind, and what does it cover?

Some of these questions might be difficult to ask, and some might be even harder for your loved one to answer. In some cases they may not have thought about the answer; if that is the case, let them use this conversation as space in which to do so. In other cases, they may tell you not to worry, say such issues are too far off, or suggest these issues are inappropriate for someone your age to think about. Gently remind them that they are very important to you and you care about them, and thus want to help them make these critical needs/wishes explicit. Finally, some people might get offended or upset with the sensitive nature of the topic. If so, show patience and understanding. Remind them that you just want to have a plan in place so that in the event something terrible happens, you can focus your energy not on first figuring out what steps to take, but how to best love and support them.

The editors have compiled the following list of organizations concerned with the issues debated in this book. The descriptions are derived from materials provided by the organizations. All have publications or information available for interested readers. The list was compiled on the date of publication of the present volume; names, addresses, phone and fax numbers, and e-mail and Internet addresses may change. Be aware that many organizations take several weeks or longer to respond to inquiries, so allow as much time as possible.

The American Life League (ALL)
PO Box 1350
Stafford, VA 22555
(540) 659-4171
e-mail: info@all.org
website: www.all.org

ALL opposes euthanasia and assisted suicide on the grounds that all of life is sacred and that it is inappropriate for human beings to take steps to end it prematurely. In addition to several newsletters and fact sheets, ALL publishes the magazine *Celebrate Life*.

American Society of Law, Medicine, and Ethics
765 Commonwealth Ave., Ste. 1634
Boston, MA 02215
(617) 262-4990
e-mail: info@aslme.org
website: www.aslme.org

This group acts as a forum for discussion of issues such as hospice care, palliative care, advance directives, euthanasia, assisted suicide, and other end-of-life issues. The society's members include physicians, attorneys, health care administrators, and others interested in the relationship between law, medicine, and ethics.

Autonomy, Inc.
14 Strawberry Hill Ln.
Danvers, MA 01923
(617) 320-0506
e-mail: info@autonomynow.org
website: www.myautonomy.org

Autonomy, Inc. represents the interests of disabled people who want legal, safe access to physician-assisted suicide. The organization also supports states' efforts to legalize physician-assisted suicide and has filed important papers in major right-to-die cases. Its website offers articles and an extensive bibliography on how euthanasia offers the disabled much-deserved control over their lives and deaths.

Compassion & Choices
PO Box 10180
Denver, CO 80250
(800) 247-7421
website: www.compassionandchoices.org

Compassion & Choices advocates end-of-life planning, palliative care, and counseling that expands people's end-of-life choices. Its website features first-person accounts, as well as the group's advocacy work in the courts.

Death with Dignity National Center
520 SW Sixth Ave., Ste. 1220
Portland, OR 97204
(503) 228-4415
e-mail: info@deathwithdignity.org
website: www.deathwithdignity.org

This group's mission is to expand end-of-life choices and advocate for the legalization of physician-assisted suicide. Its website offers articles, personal stories, and news updates that support aid in dying and euthanasia.

Dignitas
PO Box 17
8127 Forch
Switzerland
e-mail: dignitas@dignitas.ch
website: www.dignitas.ch

This controversial Swiss group, based near Zurich, counsels people with terminal illness, mental illness, and/or severe disabilities who want to die.

Dignity in Dying
181 Oxford St.
London W1D 2JT
United Kingdom
+44 (0)870 777 7868
e-mail: info@dignityindying.org.uk
website: www.dignityindying.org.uk

Formerly the Voluntary Euthanasia Society, this British group seeks to legalize physician-assisted suicide in the United Kingdom. Its mission is to secure the right for people to be able to die with dignity. In addition to information on the issue, the organization's website offers compelling stories and first-person testimonials.

Dying with Dignity
55 Eglinton Ave. East, Suite 802
Toronto, ON M4P 1G8
Canada
(800) 495-6156
e-mail: info@dyingwithdignity.ca
website: www.dyingwithdignity.ca

Dying with Dignity supports legalized physician-assisted suicide in Canada. The group also seeks to improve hospice and palliative care services. To this end, it sponsors educational and counseling services for individuals faced with making important end-of-life decisions.

Euthanasia Prevention Coalition
PO Box 25033
London, ON N6C 6A8
Canada
(877) 439-3348
e-mail: info@epcc.ca
website: www.epcc.ca

This group opposes efforts to legalize euthanasia and physician-assisted suicide. It publishes a newsletter, multiple reports, and brochures that aim to educate people about the dangers of legalizing any measures that hasten death.

Euthanasia Research & Guidance Organization (ERGO)
24829 Norris Ln.
Junction City, OR 97448-9559
(541) 998-1873
e-mail: ergo@efn.org
website: www.finalexit.org

ERGO is a nonprofit organization founded to educate patients, physicians, and the general public about euthanasia and physician-assisted suicide. The organization serves a broad range of people, providing research for students, other "right-to-die" organizations, authors, and journalists; conducting opinion polls; drafting guidelines about how to prepare for and commit assisted suicide for physicians and patients; and counseling dying patients who are competent adults in the final stages of a terminal illness.

Farewell Foundation
322-720 Sixth St.
New Westminster, BC V3L3C5
Canada
e-mail: info@farewellfoundation.ca
website: www.farewellfoundation.ca

This pro-euthanasia and pro-assisted-suicide organization believes that people have the right to make choices about their own bodies, their physical and psychological integrity, and their basic human dignity.

Final Exit Network
PO Box 665
Pennington, NJ 08534
(866) 654-915
e-mail: pr@finalexitnetwork.org
website: www.finalexitnetwork.org

This organization argues that the right to preside over one's own death is the human and civil rights cause of this century, on a par with the women's suffrage and civil rights movements of the twentieth century. Medical advances have created longer lives and, sometimes ironically, longer and more painful deaths. The organization supports laws that protect the right of every adult to a peaceful, dignified death.

Human Life International (HLI)
4 Family Life Ln.
Front Royal, VA 22630
(800) 549-5433
e-mail: hli@hli.org
website: www.hli.org

This organization opposes euthanasia and believes physician-assisted suicide is unethical. It claims that the unborn, the disabled, the ill, and the elderly are critically threatened by euthanasia and assisted suicide and provides education, advocacy, and support services on the matter.

National Hospice and Palliative Care Organization
1731 King St.
Alexandria, VA 22314
(703) 837-1500
e-mail: nhpco_info@nhpco.org
website: www.nhpco.org

The National Hospice and Palliative Care Organization believes that with proper care and pain medication, the terminally ill can live out their lives comfortably and in the company of their families. For this reason, it opposes physician-assisted suicide and works to educate the public about the benefits of hospice and palliative care for the terminally ill and their families.

National Right to Life Committee (NRLC)
512 Tenth St. NW
Washington, DC 20004
(202) 626-8800
e-mail: nrlc@nrlc.org
website: www.nrlc.org

Euthanasia and physician-assisted suicide are among the many issues opposed by the NRLC, which believes that life is sacred and deserving of protection at every stage and phase. It publishes the monthly *National Right to Life News* and many articles on end-of-life issues from a conservative perspective.

Not Dead Yet
497 State St.
Rochester, NY 146080
(585) 697-1640
website: www.notdeadyet.org

This group comprises disabled people who oppose euthanasia and physician-assisted suicide by arguing that these constitute deadly forms of discrimination against old, ill, and disabled people. It supports hospice and palliative care as the alternative to assisted suicide. Its website offers many articles, fact sheets, personal stories, and other information from an anti-euthanasia, anti-physician-assisted-suicide perspective.

Patients Rights Council
PO Box 760
Steubenville, OH 43952
(740) 282-3810
website: www.patientsrightscouncil.org

Formerly known as the International Task Force on Euthanasia and Assisted Suicide, this group combats efforts to legalize euthanasia and physician-assisted suicide. Its website offers information about end-of-life care, disability rights, pain management, advance directives, euthanasia, and physician-assisted suicide laws in various American states and foreign countries.

Physicians for Compassionate Care Education Foundation
PO Box 1933
Yakima, WA 98907
(503) 533-8154
website: www.pccef.org

This organization promotes compassionate care for severely ill patients without sanctioning or assisting their suicide. Its members believe that all human life is inherently valuable and that a physician's role is to heal illness, alleviate suffering, and provide comfort for the sick and dying.

The Right to Die Society of Canada
145 Macdonell Ave.
Toronto, ON M6R 2A4
Canada
(416) 535-0690
e-mail: info@righttodie.ca
website: www.righttodie.ca

This organization supports the right of any mature individual who is chronically or terminally ill to choose the time, place, and means of his or her death. Its publications include *Free to Go* and a regular newsletter, both of which feature pro-assisted-suicide and euthanasia articles.

BIBLIOGRAPHY

Books

Howard Ball, *At Liberty to Die: The Battle for Death with Dignity in America*. New York: New York University Press, 2012. Documents how the right of a competent, terminally ill person to die on his or her own terms with the help of a doctor has become deeply embroiled in debates about the relationship between religion, civil liberties, politics, and law in American life.

Ira Byock, *The Best Care Possible: A Physician's Quest to Transform Care Through the End of Life*. New York: Avery, 2013. One of the foremost palliative-care physicians in the country argues that the manner in which Americans die represents a national crisis.

Richard N. Cote, *In Search of Gentle Death: The Fight for Your Right to Die with Dignity*. Charleston, SC: Corinthian, 2012. Explores the modern history of the death-with-dignity movement through the lives of its founders, leaders, and activists. Features the results of five years of intensive primary-source research and more than one hundred in-depth interviews with death-with-dignity pioneers, activists, physicians, nurses, hospice workers, and their patients on four continents.

Peter H. Diamandis and Steven Kotler, *Abundance: The Future Is Better than You Think*. New York: Free, 2012. Documents how four forces—exponential technologies, the do-it-yourself innovator, the technophilanthropist, and the rising billion—are conspiring to solve humanity's biggest problems, including death.

Lee Gutkind, *At the End of Life: True Stories About How We Die*. Pittsburgh, PA: In Fact, 2012. Uses twenty-two compelling personal-medical narratives to explore death, dying, and palliative care. Highlights current features, flaws, and advances in the health care system.

Frances Norwood, *The Maintenance of Life: Preventing Social Death Through Euthanasia Talk and End-of-Life Care—Lessons from the*

Netherlands. Durham, NC: Carolina Academic, 2009. A power-ful story about how the dying, their families, and their physicians confronted this difficult subject.

John West, *The Last Goodnights: Assisting My Parents with Their Suicides*. Berkeley, CA: Counterpoint, 2010. Offers a unique and personal look inside one of the most polarizing issues of the twenty-first century: assisted suicide.

Periodicals and Internet Sources

Janet Adamy and Tom McGinty, "The Crushing Cost of Health Care," *Wall Street Journal*, July 6, 2012. http://online.wsj.com /article/SB10001424052702304441404577483050976766184 .html.

Peter B. Bach, "When Care Is Worth It, Even if End Is Death," *New York Times*, December 13, 2011. www.nytimes.com/2011/12/13 /health/policy/when-care-is-worth-it-even-if-end-is-death.html.

Jon Bardin, "For Terminal Patients, Earlier Talk About End of Life May Alter Choices," *Los Angeles Times*, November 13, 2012. http://articles.latimes.com/2012/nov/13/news/la-heb-end-of-life -early-discussions-20121113.

David Benatar, "A Legal Right to Die," *Current Oncology*, vol. 8, no. 5, 2011. www.current-oncology.com/index.php/oncology /article/view/923/751.

Earl Blumenauer, "My Near Death Panel Experience," *New York Times*, November 14, 2009. www.nytimes.com/2009/11/15 /opinion/15blumenauer.html?pagewanted=all.

J. Donald Boudreau, "Physician-Assisted Suicide Poisons the Mission of Medicine," *Globe & Mail* (Toronto, ON), August 27, 2012. www.theglobeandmail.com/commentary/physician-assisted -suicide-poisons-the-mission-of-medicine/article4503845.

Ira Byock, "Physician-Assisted Suicide Is Not Progressive," *Atlantic*, October 25, 2012. www.theatlantic.com/health/archive/2012/10 /physician-assisted-suicide-is-not-progressive/264091.

Jonathan Cohn, "Why We Don't Let People Die," *New Republic*, September 16, 2011. www.newrepublic.com/blog/jonathan

-cohn/95071/ron-paul-libertarian-health-insurance-charity
-care#.

Ken Connor, "Should Government Ration Health Care? A
Question Worth Debating," *Carroll (MD) Standard*, October 15,
2012. www.carrollstandard.com/op-ed/guest-commentary/21
602-should-government-ration-health-care-a-question-worth
-debating.

E.J. Dionne Jr., "Liberals Should Be Wary of Assisted Suicide,"
Washington Post, *Post Partisan* (blog), November 1, 2012. http://
www.washingtonpost.com/blogs/post-partisan/post/liberals
-should-be-wary-of-assisted-suicide/2012/11/01/81971b10-245e
-11e2-9313-3c7f59038d93_blog.html.

Economist, "Easing Death," October 20, 2012. www.economist
.com/news/leaders/21564849-terminally-ill-people-should-have
-right-gentle-death-right-should-not-be.

Ezekiel J. Emanuel, "Better, If Not Cheaper, Care for the Dying,"
New York Times, *Opinionator* (blog), January 3, 2013. http://opin
ionator.blogs.nytimes.com/2013/01/03/better-if-not-cheaper
-care.

Atul Gawande, "Letting Go: What Should Medicine Do When
It Can't Save Your Life?," *New Yorker*, August 2, 2010.
www.newyorker.com/reporting/2010/08/02/100802fa_fact
_gawande?currentPage=all.

John M. Grohol, "Death with Dignity: Why I Don't Want to Have
to Starve Myself to Death," PsychCentral.com, September 30,
2012. http://psychcentral.com/blog/archives/2012/09/30/death
-with-dignity-why-i-dont-want-to-have-to-starve-myself-to
-death.

Mary E. Harnud, "The Dangers of Assisted Suicide," Americans
United for Life, April 2012. www.aul.org/wp-content
/uploads/2012/04/dangers-assisted-suicide.pdf.

Sue Horton, "A Father's Day Gift: Having the End-of-Life Talk,"
Los Angeles Times, June 17, 2012. http://articles.latimes.com/2012
/jun/17/opinion/la-oe-0617-horton-end-of-life-20120617.

Nancy Houser, "The Right of Free Will for Physician-Assisted Suicide," *Digital Journal*, December 4, 2011. www.digitaljournal.com/article/315479.

Bill Keller, "How to Die," *New York Times*, October 8, 2012. www.nytimes.com/2012/10/08/opinion/keller-how-to-die.html?pagewanted=all.

Charles Krauthammer, "Government by Regulation. Shhh," *Washington Post*, December 31, 2010. www.washingtonpost.com/wp-dyn/content/article/2010/12/30/AR2010123003047.html.

Steve Lopez, "Coming to Grips with Death and Dying," *Los Angeles Times*, December 28, 2011. http://articles.latimes.com/2011/dec/28/local/la-me-1228-lopez-20111227.

Carolyn McClanahan, "Should We Ration End of Life Care?," *Forbes*, October 10, 2012. www.forbes.com/sites/carolynmcclanahan/2012/10/10/should-we-ration-end-of-life-care.

Eileen McNamara, "Death with Dignity?," *Boston Magazine*, December 2011. www.bostonmagazine.com/2011/11/death-with-dignity.

Minnesota Citizens Concerned for Life, "What's Wrong with Assisted Suicide?," *MCCL News*, November/December, 2012. http://prolifemn.blogspot.com/2013/01/whats-wrong-with-assisted-suicide.html.

Tauriq Moosa, "Why Infanticide Can Be Moral," BigThink, July 5, 2012. http://bigthink.com/against-the-new-taboo/why-infanticide-can-be-moral.

Charles Orenstein, "How Mom's Death Changed My Thinking About End-of-Life Care," Propublica, February 28, 2013. www.propublica.org/article/how-moms-death-changed-my-thinking-about-end-of-life-care.

Tadeusz Pacholczyk, "Please Step Back from the Assisted-Suicide Ledge," *Wall Street Journal*, October 7, 2012. http://online.wsj.com/article/SB10000872396390444223104578038703017615898.html.

Donald L. Pendley, "Hospice Care Offers Death with Dignity," *Courier-Post* (New Jersey), November 24, 2012. www.courier

postonline.com/article/20121125/OPINION02/311250012/Hospice-care-offers-death-dignity.

Kevin Pho, "Politics Mustn't Silence End-of-Life Talks," *USA Today*, April 12, 2011. http://usatoday30.usatoday.com/news/opinion/forum/2011-04-12-pho-end-of-life-planning.htm?loc=interstitialskip.

André Picard, "Quebec Leading the Way on End-of-Life Issues," *Globe and Mail* (Toronto, ON), January 31, 2013. www.theglobeandmail.com/life/health-and-fitness/health/andr-picard-quebec-leading-the-way-on-end-of-life-issues/article7447929.

Ronald Pies, "Merciful Assistance or Physician-Assisted Killing?," *World of Psychology* (blog), PsychCentral.com, September 30, 2012. http://psychcentral.com/blog/archives/2012/09/30/merciful-assistance-or-physician-assisted-killing.

Donald Quinn, "Obamacare and Its Impact on End-of-Life Care," *Digital Journal*, October 25, 2012. http://digitaljournal.com/article/335500.

Steven Rattner, "Health Care Reform Beyond Obamacare," *New York Times*, September 16, 2012. www.nytimes.com/2012/09/17/opinion/health-care-reform-beyond-obamacare.html?ref=todayspaper.

Murray Sabrin, "End-of-Life Care: Can We Afford It?," *Record* (Bergen County, NJ), February 28, 2010. www.northjersey.com/news/opinions/End_of_life_care_can_we_afford_it.html?page=all.

William Saletan, "After-Birth Abortion: The Pro-Choice Case for Infanticide," *Slate*, March 12, 2012. www.slate.com/articles/health_and_science/human_nature/2012/03/after_birth_abortion_the_pro_choice_case_for_infanticide.html.

David Shaywitz, "End-of-Life Medical Advice: Devaluing Patients in Name of Greater Good?," *Forbes*, June 1, 2012. www.forbes.com/sites/davidshaywitz/2012/06/01/why-we-shouldnt-dismiss-death-panels-as-pure-demagoguery.

John M. Shotwell, "Maybe Now, Nation Can Discuss Reasonableness of Assisted Suicide," Kentucky.com, June 19,

2011. www.kentucky.com/2011/06/19/1780778/maybe-now -nation-can-discuss-reasonableness.html.

Wesley J. Smith, "Why Assisted Suicide Lost in MA," *National Review*, November 7, 2012. www.nationalreview.com/human -exceptionalism/332882/why-assisted-suicide-lost-ma.

Margaret Somerville. "When Is Euthanasia Justified?," *Globe & Mail* (Toronto, ON) March 12, 2010. www.theglobeandmail.com/life /health-and-fitness/when-is-euthanasia-justified/article4392696.

Howard Swint, "End-of-Life Care Threatens Economy," *Charleston (WV) Gazette*, December 12, 2010. www.wvgazette.com /Opinion/OpEdCommentaries/201012120639.

Michael Wolff, "A Life Worth Ending," *New York*, May 20, 2012. http://nymag.com/news/features/parent-health-care-2012-5.

Peter Wolfgang, "Suicide at Life's End a Slippery, Messy Slope," *Hartford (CT) Courant*, January 11, 2013. http://articles.courant .com/2013-01- 11/news/hc-op-wolfgang-false-promise-assisted -suicide-1216-20130111_1_lethal-doses-physician-suicides.

Websites

Death with Dignity Act: Washington State Department of Health (www.doh.wa.gov/YouandYourFamily/IllnessandDisease /DeathwithDignityAct.aspx). This is the website of Washington State's Death with Dignity Act, which was passed in 2008 and went into effect in 2009. Available for download are annual reports on who takes advantage of the state's program and under what circumstances.

Euthanasia.com (www.euthanasia.com). Offers an exhaustive archive of up-to-date research materials about mercy killing, physician-assisted suicide, palliative and hospice care, euthanasia, and other end-of-life issues.

The Nightingale Alliance (www.nightingalealliance.org). This website opposes the legalization of euthanasia and physician-assisted suicide. It offers facts about the topic, current news stories, personal accounts, research papers, and more.

Oregon Department of Human Services, Death with Dignity Act (http://public.health.oregon.gov/ProviderPartnerResources /EvaluationResearch/DeathwithDignityAct/Pages/inde .aspx). This website contains a wealth of information related to Oregon's Death with Dignity Act, which has been in effect since 1997. Numerous reports are available on who has been prescribed lethal medication, when and if they have taken it, and other data.

The World Federation of Right to Die Societies (www.worldrtd .net). This group consists of forty-nine right-to-die organizations from twenty-six countries. The federation provides an international link for organizations working to secure or protect the rights of individuals to maintain self-determination at the end of their lives.

INDEX

A

Abortion, 69
Advance directives, 22, 25, 28
  percentage of doctors *vs.* general public having created, 11
Affordable Care Act. *See* Patient Protection and Affordable Care Act
Age, Medicare's spending on hospital care by, 36
American Medical Association (AMA), 47–48
Angell, Marcia, 52

B

Begg, Duncan, 72
Berwick, Donald, 28
Bloche, M. Gregg, 33
Bowron, Craig, 17, 20
Brown, Andrew, 64

C

Campanella, Linda, 57
Center for Medicare and Medicaid Services, 28
Chesterton, G.K., 28
Children, ending lives of, is never moral, 67–71
CPR (cardiopulmonary resuscitation), survival rates after, 12
Crisp, John M., 62

D

Death with Dignity Act (DWDA, OR), 55–56
  numbers of prescription recipients/deaths under, by year, *54*
Diem, Susan, 11–12
Doctor-patient relationship, physician-assisted suicide would undermine, 47–49
Dzeng, Elizabeth, 6, 8

E

End-of-life care
  economics should not influence decisions on, 27–32
  financial matters should influence decisions on, 21–26
  government should ration, 33–39
  levels of public awareness of, by country, *18*
  protocols for, 5
  should be minimal/swift, 10–15
  should not necessarily be minimal/swift, 16–20

G

Gallo, Joseph J., 11
Giubilini, Alberto, 67, 68, 69
Goold, Robert, 6–7
Government, should ration end-of-life care, 33–39

H
Harris, John, 69
Hippocratic oath, 5, 48
Hospice care
  cost of, *vs.* hospitalization, 22
  is not preferable to physician-
    assisted suicide, 62–66
  is preferable to physician-
    assisted suicide, 57–61
  length of stay in, proportion
    of patients by, 65
  number of patients served by,
    trend in, 60
  See also Palliative care
Hughes-Hallett, Thomas, 5–6

I
Infanticide, is never moral,
  67–71

J
Jacoby, Susan, 21
Jones-Nosacek, Cynthia, 16

K
Kass, Leon, 48–49
Kehl, Karen, 12
Kevorkian, Jack, 41, 42, 44
Kurzweil, Ray, 72

L
Law of Accelerating Returns,
  73
LCP (Liverpool Care Pathway
  for the Dying Patient), 5–8
Lester, Paula, 11
Liverpool Care Pathway for
  the Dying Patient (LCP),
  5–8
Living wills, 22

proportion of Americans
  with, 25
See also Advanced directives

M
Massachusetts Medical
  Society, 47–48, 57
Medicare, 17
  cost to, for per-day
    hospitalization *vs.* hospice
    care, 22
  proposed cuts in, 38
  resistance to incorporation
    of end-of-life planning into,
    28–29
  spending on hospital care by,
    by age, 36
Minerva, Francesca, 67, 68, 69
Morality
  as basis for abortion
    restrictions, 69
  of behaviors/social policies,
    opinion on, 43
Moving Toward Peace (Kehl),
  12
Murray, Ken, 10

N
Nanobot, medical, 73, 74
The Netherlands, euthanasia
  in, 49–51
Nozick, Robert, 32

O
Obama, Barack, 38
O'Malley, Seán P., 45, 48
Opinion polls. *See* Surveys

P
Palin, Sarah, 27, 32

Palliative care, 5, 6, 19
  may be inadequate for some
    patients, 53–55
  physician-assisted suicide
    would undermine, 47
  See also Hospice care
PAS. *See* Physician-assisted
  suicide
Patient Protection and
  Affordable Care Act (2010),
  22, 28, 32
Phillips, Susan, 6–7
Physician-assisted suicide
  (PAS), 42
  has safeguards to prevent
    abuse/coercion, 52–56
  legalization will lead to
    abuse/coerced death, 45–51
  states allowing, 50, 66
Polls. *See* Surveys
Pullicino, Patrick, 8

Q
Quality of life standards, 47

R
Ryan, Paul, 38

S
Savulescu, Julian, 67, 69, 71
Schumacher, J. Donald, 28,
  29
Singer, Peter, 69
Spencer, Fritz, 40
Stopa, Mike, 27
Suicide, physician-assisted
  suicide could lead to general
  increase in, 49

Surveys
  on end-of-life care, 24–25
  of doctors on medical
    technologies/interventions,
    14
  of doctors *vs.* general public
    on advance directives, 11
  on health care system
    spending to extend life, 30
  on levels of concern for end-
    of-life issues, 23
  on moral acceptability of
    behaviors/social policies, 43
  on whether doctors should
    always try to save life, 23–24

T
Technology, may allow
  humans to live forever, 72–75
Terminally ill, do not have
  right to choose when/how to
  die, 40–44
Thanatron, 41
To Live Each Day with Dignity
  (US Council of Catholic
  Bishops), 49
Tooley, Michael, 69

U
US Council of Catholic
  Bishops, 49

V
Van Hock-Burgerhart, Elise,
  51

W
Wise, Barbara, 63
Wise, John, 63, 64